The Hazardous Homestead

The Hazardous Homestead

Karen Ball

Tyndale House Publishers, Inc.
Wheaton, Illinois

Books in the Choice Adventures series

Library of Congress Cataloging-in-Publication Data

Ball, Karen, date
    The hazardous homestead / Karen Ball.
        p.   cm. — (Choice adventures ; #8)
    Summary: The reader's choices decide the course of the action when a
group of friends discover that someone is dumping toxic wastes near the ranch
they are visiting.
    ISBN 0-8423-5032-2
    1. Plot-your-own stories.   [1. Plot-your-own stories.
2. Hazardous waste—Fiction.   3. Christian life—Fiction.
4. Adventure and adventurers—Fiction.]   I. Title.   II. Series.
PZ7.B1988Haz   1992
[Fic]—dc20   91-36439

Printed in the United States of America

99 98 97 96 95 94 93 92
 9   8   7   6   5   4   3   2   1

To my brothers, Kirk and Kevin. Thanks, guys, for being my friends. And to Benjemen Leighton. Welcome to the family!

Thanks to Don for his unending (well, almost) patience and stories; Laura Burk and Peggy Whitson for their input; Jack Kasky at Garbage magazine for his assistance.

"**G**et ready! They're coming at us again!"

Suddenly the sky lit up with laser blasts and rocket fire. Willy barked out orders to his men, and they scrambled to obey. They knew the score. They were being invaded by hostile nonterrestrial life forms—and they were getting clobbered. Their only hope for survival was to do what Willy told them. He was the most trusted tactical defense specialist in the galaxy, and everyone knew it.

"Move it!" Willy yelled, grabbing up a laser blaster and preparing for the ground offensive. This was the worst battle he'd been in yet. Sweat poured down his face, stinging his eyes. He ignored it. No way would he let the fish-faced Antherians waltz in and take over the earth. . . .

RIIINGGG!

. . . not while he was around to . . .

RIIINGGG!

. . . to . . .

RIIINGGG!

Willy sat up in bed with a jolt. Dazed, he looked around. The phone beside his bed was ringing insistently. A quick glance at the clock told him it was all of seven o'clock in the morning. "Oh . . . man!" he moaned. With a groan he flopped back against the pillows.

RIIINGGG!

2

And just when he was about to save the whole world and preserve life as we know it. . . .

RIIINGGG!

He pulled his pillow over his head. He'd *told* his friends he was going to sleep in today.

Willy had done this at least once every summer vacation for the last three or four years. He would stock up on ten or twelve science-fiction books on a Friday and then read into Saturday morning until his eyes started seeing triple. He always had great dreams when he finally gave in to sleep. It was kind of his chance to live in the wonders of the future.

He'd warned his friends not to call him before ten at the earliest. So who . . . ?

RIIINGGG!

Chris.

Willy peered over his pillow unbelievingly. It had to be! Sure, the one person he hadn't told not to call him had been Chris. But he hadn't been too worried about that—Chris didn't even believe there was life before nine or ten.

RIINGGG!

With a sigh, Willy reached over and grabbed the phone. "Yeah?" he barked.

"Willy! Finally! I didn't think you'd ever answer. Where were you? On Mars?"

"I was sleeping, Chris. It just seemed the thing to do at seven o'clock in the morning." Willy's voice was dripping with sarcasm. Chris didn't even notice. He was too excited.

"Well, now that you're awake, get up! We're having a meeting at the Freeze. I've got some great news—"

3

"At the Freeze?" Willy said with a frown. "Chris, the Freeze doesn't even open until—"

"Yeah, I know. But I wanted to make sure you'd be there! You won't want to miss—"

"Chris, you're nuts," Willy said matter-of-factly. He struggled to control the urge he had to slam the phone down and leave his friend with his ears ringing. "You call me three hours early for some—"

"Three hours early?"

"Yes! This is post-sci-fi-Friday Saturday. Ten o'clock, remember?"

There was a pause. Then, "Nobody told me—"

"You're nuts anyway! Seven o'clock and you call me for some goofy meeting, wake me out of a great dream where I'm saving the world, which means the Antherians probably creamed us and we'll all have to learn how to live underwater and eat fish eyes—have you ever eaten fish eyes, Chris? They're gross! OK?—and you expect me to be excited about it?" Willy's volume had risen as he talked until he was practically yelling.

The moment of silence that followed his outburst made Willy smile with some satisfaction. Chris must be realizing what a dorf he'd been. Then a hoot of laughter jumped out of the receiver and erased Willy's smile.

"You were *what?*" Chris said, the words almost strangled by his laughter. "Saving the world? Fish eyes? When did you ever eat fish eyes? What—"

"Forget it, Chris!" Willy interrupted, suddenly feeling embarrassed. He could hear Chris laughing so hard he was starting to snort. Willy threw himself back against his pillows again. Life just isn't fair.

"Listen, Willy," Chris said, trying to control his laughter—and succeeding except for a few small snorts—*"(Mpfb!)* When you're done with your nonterrestrials—*snicker! snicker!*—and your fish eyes (do you eat those with milk or what?) come on over to the Freeze—*mpfb! snicker!*—I really do have some great news . . . provided, of course, we're all still alive to hear it!" And he was off again, laughing and snorting.

"Right. Great. I'll be there," Willy said, and he hung up. He covered his eyes with his arms and sighed.

"I wonder if the Antherians would take defectors?" he muttered angrily. One thing was for sure. He was *not* going to that meeting. He didn't care how great Chris's news was. He wasn't giving that phone-calling snorter a chance to make fun of him in front of the rest of the gang.

Then again, Chris had made a special point to call him. And he had been pretty excited. . . . What if he missed out on something really terrific?

"Aarghh!" Willy groaned in frustration. He grabbed his pillow and pulled it back over his head.

CHOICE ➤

If Willy decides not to go to the meeting, turn to page 54.

If he calls another Ringer to see if he can discover what Chris's news is, turn to page 43.

If he goes to the meeting, turn to page 23.

"**O**h boy, a roller coaster!" Jim said. He pointed at a huge, twisting ride. "The Demon! Let's start with that!" Willy quickly agreed. Pete, on the other hand, held back. Willy looked at him curiously.

"What's up?" he asked.

"I don't feel like starting out with that," Pete said, looking at the twisting frame of steel that the cars were racing along.

"Don't tell me you're afraid?" Jim said, his voice teasing. Pete felt his face turn red.

"Of course I'm not afraid!" he shot back. And that was true. Pete wasn't scared. Panic stricken, maybe. Scared spitless, definitely. Rooted to the spot in abject terror, you bet. But afraid? Nah.

The question was, did he tell his friends that or just go on the ride?

CHOICE ➤

If Pete goes on the roller coaster, turn to page 85.

If he doesn't, turn to page 133.

6

"I think we'd better stick to the path," Pete finally said. "We don't know what's making that sound or how far away it is."

"OK," Jill said wearily. She knew they were passing up a possible adventure, but she was too tired to care. They started out again, trudging along on the dusty path. About half an hour later, Pete suddenly gave a little cheer and grabbed Jill's arm.

"Look!" he said, pointing in front of them. She looked in that direction and caught her breath. A break in the woods! And just beyond, she could see the fence!

"All right!" she said, and the two ran out of the woods. It took them another half hour of walking before they ran into Uncle Fred and some of the others who were out looking for them. The Ringers gathered around their friends, hugging them and slapping them on the back.

Uncle Fred looked at the two tired friends and took charge. "OK, you kids. Everybody into the truck. Pete and Jill, you ride up front with me. The rest of you can hop in back. They can tell us all their story after they've had a chance to clean up and get some food."

Several hours later, the whole gang sat in the living room. It was a warm evening, so they were all sipping lemonade.

"Man!" Sam said for the twentieth time. "I was beginning to think we'd never find you guys."

"Well, I'm glad you did," Jill said, smiling.

"Yeah," Pete remarked. "And I'm glad we didn't try to find out what that sound in the woods was."

Uncle Fred looked at Pete curiously. "Sound in the woods?" he asked, looking from Pete to Jill. They explained what they had heard and how they had debated as to whether or not to follow it.

"Hmmm," Uncle Fred said thoughtfully. "I'll have to have someone check it out. But right now," he said, noticing Jill's droopy eyes and Pete's yawn, "I think you two adventurers should hit the hay."

The next morning, the fence repair crew was surprised to find the calf that had run away the day before standing outside the fence they had repaired, trying to find a way back inside. He looked lost and lonely. Fortunately, his was the only attempted escape the kids had to deal with.

The rest of the week went by quickly. Before the Ringers knew it, it was time to head for home. They thanked Uncle Fred and Aunt Paula for their hospitality and promised to come back again.

It wasn't until weeks later that the Ringers heard from Uncle Fred again. Chris came bursting into the Freeze one afternoon and called a meeting of the Ringers. When they had all gathered together, he told them that Uncle Fred had told the local authorities about the sound Pete and Jill heard in the woods. When the police checked the area out, they had discovered that someone was dumping toxic wastes in a creek deep in the woods! They had reported the whole thing to the regional EPA authorities, who then had conducted a big undercover investigation. The people and companies involved in the illegal dumping had been caught and arrested just in the last week.

"Oh my gosh!" Jill said, shocked. She looked at Pete and shook her head. "Now *that* would have been some adventure! Catching someone dumping toxic waste!"

"Oh, I don't know," Pete said, grinning at her. "Sounds to me like it could have been a real *waste* of time." The others groaned and threw napkins and wadded up paper at Pete, which resulted in an all-out paper-ball war.

But in the midst of the laughter and play, several of the Ringers wished they'd been in on the discovery and arrest of the perpetrators. They hated to think that they'd missed out on such a great adventure!

THE END

If you haven't found out who's doing the illegal dumping, turn to page 92.

Or, turn to page 14.

Sam took a deep breath, then nodded.

"OK," he said, stepping forward and offering Uncle Fred his hand to shake on it. "You've got a deal. I'll give it a shot for two days."

"All right!" Chris said, grinning. "Let's get that luggage into the house!"

"Under one condition," Sam added. He paused for effect. "I don't have to physically touch any manure."

They laughed. "We're going to make you *brush your teeth* with manure, dude!" said Willy.

"Oh . . . *sick!*" said Jill. With disgusted looks, they all headed for the house.

Turn to page 30.

Pete argued with himself for a few moments then finally made a decision. He would wait for five minutes. If Willy, Sam, and Jim didn't show up in that time, he would go without them.

Just then he heard Willy's voice. "Hey, buddy! How was the wheel?" Pete spun around and saw his two friends walking toward him.

"It was great!" he said, and he quickly explained what he had seen.

"Well, what are we waiting for?" Jim said. "Let's go catch us a milkman!"

The four boys ran to the carnival booths, dodging in and out of the crowds of people. Finally, they reached the booth Pete had seen. It was a ring-toss booth, with all kinds of milk bottles set out for people to try to throw rings over.

After catching their breath, the boys agreed on a plan. Pete and Jim would stroll around the booth toward the back, where they'd try to get the license number of the truck. Willy and Sam would get in line at the booth and see if they could find out anything by talking with the guy who was running it.

Pete and Jim walked as casually as they could toward the back of the booth. The truck was still there! Jim snuck to the back of the truck to write down the license number while Pete stood watch. Suddenly a man came walking toward the truck. Pete looked at him and gasped. It was one of the gun-toting guards from the creek!

The man looked at Pete suspiciously. "What are you doing here, kid?" he growled.

"Just waiting for my friend," Pete said, trying to sound casual. "Oh, there he is!" he said as Jim came from behind the truck. The man's eyes narrowed.

"What were you doing back there?" he said.

"I was just looking around," Jim answered quickly.

"Yeah, well, there's nothin' to see back here. So you kids get lost!" Pete and Jim were only too glad to do so. They hurried back to the front, where Willy and Sam already were waiting for them.

"Did you get the license number?" Sam asked them.

"You bet!" Jim said.

"Yeah, and something else," Pete said, then told them about the man.

"Well, listen to this!" Willy said. "The people sponsoring this booth are none other than Mitchell Chemical Supply, an area chemical producer! I don't know about you guys, but I think we've got some pretty helpful information to give the sheriff now."

They headed for the animal exhibits, where they knew Uncle Fred and Aunt Paula were with the other Ringers. Once they found them and explained what had happened, they went to a phone where Uncle Fred called the sheriff. Within a half hour he pulled up to where the group was waiting, and the kids filled him in on all they'd discovered.

The sheriff shook his head and gave a low whistle. "You kids ever need a job, just give me a call," he said. "I could use more investigators like you."

"So you think this chemical company is really who's been doing the dumping?" Tina asked.

The sheriff nodded thoughtfully. "I can't say for sure, but things do look bad for them—especially since we've had trouble with them meeting safety and waste-management requirements before. At any rate, I appreciate your help. I'll let you know what comes of it."

It wasn't until several weeks later that the Ringers finally heard what had happened. Chris had heard from his mom, who had heard from Uncle Fred, who had heard from the sheriff. The regional EPA authorities had done an investigation and found evidence that the chemical company was indeed dumping waste in the woods. The people and companies involved in the illegal dumping had been caught and arrested.

The Ringers exploded with excitement, yelling and giving each other high-fives.

"All right!"

"Way to go, Pete and Jill!"

"Move over Perry Mason!"

"Another bad guy *wasted!*"

Betty Metz came walking up then carrying a tray full of milkshakes. "I'm proud of you guys. How about some complimentary milkshakes to celebrate the capture of those environmental assassins?"

She was met with enthusiasm. After the shakes had all

been handed around, Tina looked at Betty curiously. "Why did you call those guys 'environmental assassins,' Betty?"

"Because that's what they are. When someone does something like dumping toxic waste, they're killing the environment. The funny thing is that people who do those things seem to think they can keep using up or damaging the earth and never pay for it."

"Well, they don't unless they get caught," Jim said.

Betty shook her head. "I'm not so sure, Jim. Whether we learn to care for the earth or not, the planet will go on. But the *life* on it won't. We can't survive without air or water or soil. So we all end up paying for what's happening."

"I never really thought of it that way," Willy said. "I guess it's not just the earth's future that's at stake."

"I'm afraid not," Betty said, lifting the now-empty tray. "It's more our future that's at stake."

"Well, God *did* tell Adam and Eve that they were supposed to take care of the world and all that was on it, right?" Jill said.

"Right," the others echoed.

"OK, then, what say we get serious about taking on the project Aunt Paula suggested," Jill continued. "There are plenty of things we can do to make a change in our own homes—"

"And in Millersburg," Pete added.

Betty smiled at them. "Sounds like a plan to me," she said.

THE END
Turn to page 143.

14

Have you found out about the milk truck yet? If not, turn back to the beginning and make other choices. Follow the adventures of the Ringers gang until you too discover why it's a *hazardous* homestead!

Jill followed Pete's trail cautiously, trying not to make any sound. She finally spotted him, crouching behind a large bush. She crept up beside him and glanced over his shoulder. They could see the truck more clearly now.

When he finally got a clear view, Pete was startled to see a large hose coming out of the back of the truck. The men in the strange "space suits" were standing nearby, watching as something was pumped from the truck, through the hose, into the creek. Pete could see that the clear water of the creek was being colored by whatever was coming out of the truck. It almost looked as though there were some kind of oil in the water. There was also a foam forming on the top of the water.

"Oh, man!" Pete said, sitting back, his voice sounding alarmed. "They're dumping something into that creek." He looked at Jill.

She could see he was really spooked. "Dumping something?" she echoed. "Like what?"

"I don't know a lot about dairy farming," he said, "but I'm willing to bet that isn't old milk!"

Jill stretched up and looked over the bush. She noted the hose, the men, and the foaming water. She sat back frustrated. "What do you think is going on?" she asked Pete in a whisper.

He looked at her, his eyes solemn. "I don't know, not

for sure. But I remember now where I've seen suits like those guys are wearing. Sam and I did a report once on industrial waste disposal. He brought some of his dad's industrial magazines for us to look through. In this one magazine we saw lots of ads for suits just like those guys are wearing. I remember we laughed about how goofy they looked. Just like spacemen. . . ."

Jill didn't like the tone of Pete's voice. He sounded like he was leading up to some bad news. Some real bad news. "So what were the suits for?" she asked.

"They were for protection when you handle some kinds of hazardous waste."

"'Hazardous waste?'" Jill echoed, shocked. She looked in the direction of the truck. "You mean, those guys are dumping toxic waste into that creek?"

"I don't know," Pete snapped. "But they sure aren't wearing those suits to keep from getting sunburned!"

Jill felt tears smart at her eyes. "What are we going to do?" she asked Pete in a choked voice. "We can't just keep hiding here. We're already an hour late for lunch and I'm *starving*. And besides, we don't know how long these guys are gonna be here, and we don't know where we are, and we can't stay in the woods all night, and—"

"OK, OK," Pete said, trying to calm her down. "Just give me a minute here. I'll think of something." Actually, he had two ideas in mind already. He just wasn't sure which one was safest. They could try to follow the truck out of the woods when it finally left. But there was no telling how much longer they would be dumping. If they didn't leave until after dark, would he and Jill be able to follow them?

Or they could just go back to the overgrown path they'd been following before.

"Jill," he said at last, "I think we should pray about this."

"I have been," she answered. "Remember that Bible verse, 'Ask and you shall receive'? Well, ever since we got lost, I've been asking God to help us. So I know we'll be OK."

Pete looked at her and nodded.

Then they bowed their heads. Pete whispered, "Lord, please help us make a good choice right now."

CHOICE ➤

If they follow the truck, turn to page 95.

If they go back to the path, turn to page 69.

18

"This is going to be a blast!" Chris said, grinning at his friends as they watched the landscape go by out the windows of the van. They were only about a half hour away from the ranch.

Jill had been watching the changes in the scenery. All around them were rolling hills and fields that seemed to stretch on forever. In the distance, Jill could see forests. She wished she could get out and take a walk in those woods. She was sure she'd be able to spot some deer or other wildlife.

Pete stretched his arms and yawned, then looked at Chris. "Yeah," he said in response to Chris's enthusiastic comment. "A real blast. A whole week on a ranch to do nothing but slop pigs, milk cows, cut hay, shovel out the barn—"

"Whoa! Hold on there!" Sam said, settling back in his seat and crossing his arms. "Nobody said anything about cleaning out barns!"

Chris aimed an eyebrow at Sam, then said in his best John Wayne imitation, "Wahl now, buck-a-roo, you knew when you signed on for this here job that you was a-gonna be helping out with the ranchin' chores. And that thar barn just ain't gonna get cleaned out by i'self."

"Yeah, Sam," Willy said with a wink. "There's no such thing as a self-cleaning barn."

"Hmpf!" Sam snorted. He knew the others were just teasing, but suddenly he wasn't so sure he'd made the right choice about coming. He'd never even seen a ranch before, let alone worked on one. Chris and the others had made it sound like fun. But now . . .

Sam tried to picture himself in the barn, shoveling manure, wearing smelly clothes, with mud and who knows what else caked on his shoes. He frowned. Maybe he should just tell Mr. Whitehead that he was going to go back home with him.

Moments later, the van turned down a gravel road. Chris was bouncing on his seat, pointing out things left and right.

"There's a creek over there where we catch crawdads and some granddaddy-sized bass. The hayfield is over that way. The red barn is where they store the hay, and it's also the stable. That smaller white barn is where the cattle are milked. Oh yeah! That tree over there has a great tire swing on it. I went so high on it once that I thought I was going into orbit!"

"Yeah, well, you're pretty spaced out right now," Sam quipped.

As soon as the van pulled to a stop, the Ringers piled out. Willy looked around, smelling the clear, sweet air. This sure wasn't city air! Jim and Tina jumped out and stretched, looking around with interest.

"Wow!" Tina said, her eyes shining with excitement. "This smells a little like Brazil!"

"I'll say!" Jim said in agreement as he hopped out of the van. "This is great!" He and Tina always seemed to be noticing things that reminded them of their childhood in South America.

A large, white, two-story ranch house was in front of them. It had a screened-in porch that looked as though it surrounded the house. Close by was a large building of wood and chicken wire. A chicken coop!

"Check out the chickens!" Willy said, pointing. Pete and Jill looked over and saw the hens walking around, scratching at the ground and losing feathers everywhere.

"All right!" Jill said, grinning. "I bet we'll get to gather eggs!"

"What do you mean 'we'?" Pete said teasingly. "I've always said I'd never let anyone henpeck me. And I'm not giving one of those feather-balls a chance to try!"

To the left of the house was the large red barn Chris had pointed out. A good-sized paddock, the fenced-in area for the horses, was next to it, and just a little beyond that was the milking house. All around the kids could hear the sounds of animals.

"That's the paddock we're going to paint," said Chris.

"Well," said Sam, "that ought to be a quick job. How long can it take to paint a padlock?" He got several glares from the others until they realized from his smile that he had been kidding.

Jim nudged Willy and grinned. "This place looks like it came straight out of 'Bonanza'!"

"Yeah," Willy agreed. "I wouldn't be surprised to see good ol' Hoss Cartwright come walking up."

"Uncle Fred! Aunt Paula!" Jim and Willy looked up to see Chris going to meet a large man coming toward them.

For a second Willy was startled—it *was* Hoss Cartwright!
Then a second look and he realized that the man was
leaner than Hoss, though he was tall. He was broad
shouldered, and as he took off his hat Willy saw that his
crew-cut hair was dark and peppered with white. The man
reached out to shake Chris's hand, engulfing the boy's
hand in his own. Chris wasn't short, but next to this guy, he
looked like a midget!

Uncle Fred would have been a pretty intimidating
figure, except for one thing. Even from a distance, Willy
could see that the man's blue eyes radiated good humor.

At Fred's side was a woman who was at least a foot
shorter. She had the same salt and pepper hair, but hers
curled softly around her face. As she reached out to hug
Chris, Willy thought she looked warm and friendly. Like
she smiled and laughed a lot.

"Guys," Chris said turning to his friends, "meet Uncle
Fred and Aunt Paula."

"We're so pleased you all could come," Aunt Paula
said with a smile. "We want you to feel comfortable here,
so please just call us Aunt Paula and Uncle Fred. We're
looking forward to your stay."

"I'll say," Uncle Fred agreed. "I've been saving the
chores for you for days." He winked at Chris. "The barn's
so full you can hardly walk through it."

Chris laughed and Aunt Paula just shook her head.
"Oh, Fred!" she said in a scolding tone. "Let them at least
get their things to their rooms before you put a shovel in
their hands!"

22

At the word *shovel*, Sam, who had been hauling baggage out of the van, froze.

"Hey, get moving, Sam!" Jill said as she bumped into him. Sam stepped aside, frowning.

"What's up, Sam?" He looked up to see Mr. Whitehead watching him.

"I . . . uh, well . . . ," Sam stammered, trying to decide what to do. Mr. Whitehead laid a hand on his shoulder and smiled at him.

"Sam," he said, "would you like to take a walk and talk?"

CHOICE ⇒

If Sam tells Mr. Whitehead what's bothering him, turn to page 88.

If he doesn't let it bother him, turn to page 71.

The Ringers gathered at the Freeze, their favorite ice-cream parlor and hangout. Willy and Pete had arrived at about the same time, and they'd slid into a large booth. Not long afterward, Jill came in. Pete smiled at her as she slid in next to him. As a rule, he didn't like being around girls too much. But Jill was OK. She seemed to know a lot about electronics and science. Considering how much she knew, Pete had been surprised to find out that she was only thirteen—a year younger than he was.

"Whew!" Jill said, fanning herself with the menu. "It may only be eight o'clock in the morning, but it's hot!"

"I'll say," Pete agreed. "But I've got a better way than that to cool off." He finished with a smile as he snatched the menu out of her hand.

"Sounds like a plan to me," a voice said. The three friends looked up to see Sam, another Ringer, sauntering toward their booth. Willy slid over to make room for him. They all studied the menu and placed their orders with Betty, the owner of the Freeze. She was about the same age as most of the kids' parents, but the Ringers all considered her a friend.

"So where are Jim and Tina?" Sam asked, licking his lips as Betty set their orders in front of them.

"Yeah, and where's Chris?" Willy asked pointedly,

losing interest for a minute in his ice cream creation. "I mean, wasn't this whole meeting his idea?"

"Jim and Tina are at the church helping Mr. Whitehead," Jill said. Mr. Whitehead was Jim and Tina's grandfather. He and his wife were retired missionaries. They had recently come to Millersburg to reopen an old church. That was where the gang had met the Whiteheads and Jim and Tina, who were living with their grandparents so they could attend school in the U.S. Jim and Tina's parents were missionaries in Brazil.

"As for Mr. Mysterious," Sam remarked, "here comes Chris!" The others looked around just as Chris burst in through the door. He was grinning at his friends and waving a piece of paper in the air over his head.

"Who's ready for change?" Chris said, a big grin on his face as he came up and slapped Willy on the back in excitement.

Willy, who had just taken a huge mouthful of his super-duper-hot-fudge-marshmallow-cream-lotsa-nuts-four-scoop sundae choked and gasped and spit ice cream all over the table. Sam, who was sitting beside him, scrambled out of the way. Jill and Pete, who had been sitting across from Willy, dove for cover, knocking Jill's milkshake and Pete's soda over in the process. Chris stepped back with a rueful grin.

"Well, Willy, that's not exactly what I had in mind," he said.

Willy shot Chris a look custom designed to kill (or at least wound significantly). "Yeah, well, choking on mocha and blueberry ice cream isn't *my* idea of a good time either," he sputtered, wiping at his face with a napkin.

"What I want to know," Jill broke in, coming up from where she'd ducked under the table, a dribble of chocolate milkshake running down her forehead, "is who's gonna clean up this mess."

"Two guesses," Betty Metz remarked as she came up to the table and handed a small bowl of water and a washcloth to Chris.

"Why me?" Chris protested. If there was one thing he hated, it was cleaning up messes. Especially someone else's!

The other kids looked at Chris accusingly, and he turned red.

CHOICE ➤

If Chris refuses to clean the table, turn to page 106.

If he agrees, turn to page 80.

"**N**ow remember," Aunt Paula said as she started clearing the table, "we leave for the fair at five o'clock tomorrow morning. That'll mean an early rise to get the chores done first."

"All right!" said the Ringers, looking and sounding like veteran ranch hands.

The night was short, but the excitement level was high by the time the gang arrived at the fairgrounds the next day.

"We can go around in a group, or split up," Uncle Fred said, and they all gathered around him.

"Let's split up," Pete suggested. "I know we'll want to see different things."

"Everyone agree?" Uncle Fred asked. They all nodded. "OK, well, the main attractions are the rides and the animal exhibits. Who wants to start with what?"

After some negotiating, they finally decided. Jill, Chris, and Tina wanted to see the animals first. Pete, Sam, Jim, and Willy wanted to start at the rides. Uncle Fred and Aunt Paula decided to go with Jill, Chris, and Tina to see the animals.

CHOICE ⇒

If you want to see which rides the boys go on, turn to page 5.

If you want to find out about the animals at the fair, turn to page 45.

"**H**ead for the fence!" Jim yelled. Jill and Pete started running for the gap, hoping to reach it before the calf did.

The calf pulled up short when it saw the kids heading for the break in the fence. It didn't know what was happening. All it knew was that it didn't want anything to do with those creatures! It spun around and raced back to the safety of the other cattle as fast as its spindly legs could carry it.

Jim, Jill, and Pete let out a cheer. Then they fixed the broken section of fence in record time. Satisfied that they'd taken care of everything they could for now, they loaded up their supplies and headed back to the house for lunch.

By the second day, they had established a routine. They had decided to do the best job they could on mending the fence, so they carefully checked each post and section. Even slightly loose boards got renailed. Uncle Fred, as all the gang called him, was impressed and delighted with their work.

The rest of the week went by quickly. They all went to the fair on Friday and had a blast. Before long it was time to go home, and Mr. Whitehead was driving up in the van. As they loaded their gear, the gang talked about all they had learned during the week. Sam was especially pleased at the gross stories he had to tell his sisters!

Uncle Fred and Aunt Paula thanked the gang for all

their help. "Any time you want to volunteer again, or even just come for a visit, you're always welcome," Uncle Fred said as the last of them climbed into the van.

"We'll be back. You can count on that!" Chris called, waving as they pulled away.

As they drove out the same gravel lane they had arrived on, the whole gang fell silent for a few moments. Sitting in the backseat, Jim, Jill, and Pete gazed out on the fences they had so carefully repaired. They smiled at each other, and Jill stuck out her hands, palms up. Her teammates on the fence-fixing team slapped her five. Then they began to compare each other's calluses and blisters.

"Sounds like you had a good time," Mr. Whitehead said, breaking the silence.

"We did," Jill said. "But the time sure went fast."

"Yeah. I'm only sorry about one thing," Pete said. The others looked at him curiously.

"This is one of the first trips we've gone on without finding a real adventure!"

"Oh, I don't know," Willy said with a grin. "You should have seen Sam with that manure spreader. . . . Now *that* was an adventure—" he broke off when a pillow nailed him in the back of the head. Everyone broke into laughter, then started sharing their stories with Mr. Whitehead.

THE END
Turn to page 14.

The afternoon went by quickly. Uncle Fred took the Ringers on a tour of the small ranch. After the tour, they all gathered in the living room to decide how to split up the work that needed to be done. Aunt Paula passed out the iced tea while Uncle Fred sat down in a big recliner and outlined what he had in mind.

"OK, here's the plan. We've got three different big projects to work on while you're here. First, we need to bale the hay. I figure that will take two of you, and I'll work with that group since we'll be running machinery. Second, we need the fence around the fields and grazing land mended and painted. That will probably be a job for three. The last job is taking care of the milking, feeding the horses, and doing all the other regular chores so we don't fall behind. Aunt Paula will help those of you who decide to do that.

"I figure we'll work steady for the next five days, except for church tomorrow, of course. Then we have a surprise for you."

"What surprise?" Chris asked.

"Well, the county fair starts on Friday. There are a lot of fun things to see and do there, and it would be a nice way to wind up your visit here."

Everyone agreed that sounded like a good plan. Then they got down to business and split into the work groups.

Willy and Sam volunteered to work with Uncle Fred baling the hay. Pete, Jim, and Jill decided to work on the fences. Which left Tina and Chris to help Aunt Paula with milking and the other chores.

"OK, gang," Uncle Fred said with a smile, "let's get started. We have just enough time before dinner to show you what you'll need to do."

With that they all headed outside.

Uncle Fred led Pete, Jim, and Jill over to a small John Deere lawn mower/tractor. It was hooked up to a small trailer with paint, brushes, cleaning supplies, tools, and boards for fence repairs in it. Uncle Fred gave each of the Ringers a pair of sturdy gloves and showed them how to remove any bad sections of the fence and replace them with new boards. Next he showed them how to operate the tractor. They took turns driving it around in a small circle and backing it up.

"OK," Uncle Fred said after watching them all try, "you're all set. All you'll need to do is drive the tractor alongside the fence, watching for places that are damaged or that have rotted. When you find one, replace the board and paint it, like I showed you."

"No problem," Pete said with confidence. Uncle Fred smiled at them.

"One other thing," he added. "Be on the lookout for any stray calves or cattle. It's getting to be the time of year when they will head in from the grazing fields. If possible, I'd like to avoid losing any of them through a broken section of fence. The surrounding woods are pretty dense, and we always have a heck of a time finding strays once they've wandered in there."

"We'll do our best," Jill told him.

He put a hand on her shoulder. "I know that, Jill."

"Do you want to show us how to run the machinery we'll be using on Monday?" Sam asked.

Uncle Fred thought for a moment, then shook his head. "I think we'll just wait until Monday morning. That way you can learn as you work. In the meantime, what do you say we go gather some blackberries for dessert tonight? Paula makes the best blackberry cobbler in the world. All we need to do is give her a bucketful, and we'll be cruisin' to blackberry heaven."

"Lead me to 'em!" Pete said, licking his lips.

Chris and Tina were following Aunt Paula around the barn as she showed them where everything was. Chris peered into one of the stalls, admiring the large, powerful horse that stood there, quietly munching grain from his feed bucket.

"He's some horse," Tina said from behind Chris. She was looking over his shoulder.

"He's new since I was here last," Chris said.

Aunt Paula nodded. "That's Topaz. Your uncle saw him at an auction and fell in love with him. He's a wonderful horse, with stamina and power that won't quit. But he's got a stubborn streak in him. Your uncle is the only one who can ride him. I pretty much steer clear of him. You kids should be careful when you go in to feed him." She smiled when Tina looked at her in alarm. "It's

OK, Tina," she reassured her. "Topaz isn't mean, he's just spirited."

"I'll feed him," Chris said, looking at the horse with appreciation. *Man, what I wouldn't give to ride that animal!*

Next, Aunt Paula showed Chris and Tina a small distiller that Uncle Fred had put together to make fuel for the farm equipment. She showed them how to mix the corn with water, then leave it to cook overnight. The end result was an alcohol-based farm fuel and some high-protein leftovers that the cattle absolutely loved.

"Isn't this like a still?" Chris asked, as he put in the amount of corn Aunt Paula had shown him.

She laughed. "It isn't *like* a still, Chris, it *is* a still. That's just a shortened term for a distiller. But we're not making liquor. The alcohol portion either goes into the fuel, or it burns off—which is a good thing, because I'd hate to have our cattle getting tipsy."

Aunt Paula showed Chris and Tina where they stored the gas that cooked the fuel, and how to refill it when it got low. Chris volunteered to take care of the gas while they were at the ranch.

That evening, Uncle Fred and Aunt Paula kept the Ringers entertained with stories about the ranch and the animals. Aunt Paula fixed a great dinner, complete with the promised blackberry cobbler for dessert. The whole gang ate until they couldn't move. It wasn't too long before the fresh air and the food did their work, and the Ringers were sitting around yawning. Uncle Fred's suggestion that they make an early night of it so they could get started early the

34

next day was accepted willingly. The chores still had to be done—even on Sunday! So they all went to their rooms.

They all slept soundly until morning.

CHOICE

Turn to page 59.

Finally, just as Jill was beginning to wonder if there *was* an end to the woods, she saw a thinning of the trees ahead. The car and truck accelerated and soon were out of sight. Pete and Jill waited a few more minutes then stepped out of the woods onto a rural road.

"Thank God!" Jill said.

"Amen to that," Pete agreed, looking around. Then he grabbed Jill's arm. "Someone's coming!" He said. Jill looked up to see a vehicle coming their way.

"It's a sheriff's car!" she exclaimed in excitement, and she and Pete ran toward the car, waving and yelling for it to stop. Which it did—along with the pickup truck that was following close behind.

"Hey," Pete said, stopping short, "that looks like—"

"Uncle Fred's pickup!" Jill finished for him. Sure enough, no sooner had the vehicles stopped than Chris, Willy, Sam, and Jim hopped out and came running toward their friends. Uncle Fred followed them, a concerned but relieved look on his face. He worked his way through the group of friends who were firing questions left and right at Jill and Pete. Finally he managed to reach them, taking in their torn and dirty appearance and the fatigue on their faces.

"I sure am glad to see you two," he said with a smile. "Are you all right?" When they nodded, he slipped an arm around their shoulders. "Thank God! It seems like we've been out looking for you for hours. I knew we'd find you, but I'm mighty glad it was so soon and that you're OK." He looked at the sheriff, who had gotten out of his car and was standing nearby, grinning and watching the reunion.

"Thanks for your help, Jack," Uncle Fred said. "It looks as though everything will be OK."

"Yer sure enough welcome, Fred," the sheriff replied good-naturedly, then headed back toward his squad car.

"Wait a minute!" Jill said, grabbing Uncle Fred's sleeve. "Don't let the sheriff leave! We have to tell him about the spacemen!" Uncle Fred looked at her in surprise.

"Spacemen?" Chris exclaimed, looking at Jill as though she'd gone totally loony. "What spacemen?"

"The ones in the dairy truck," Jill said, then turned several shades of red when Chris and Willy let out a hoot of laughter.

"Spacemen in a dairy truck!" Willy said with a grin. "Now I've heard everything!"

"Yeah," Chris added, "what were they doing? 'Milking' someone for information?"

"Nah," Sam chimed in. "They probably were planning how they were going to 'cream' us earthlings."

Jill glared at them, tired and angry.

"Knock it off, you guys," Pete finally said. "She's right. Or at least, she's kind of right." The others looked at them, shaking their heads. Pete just sighed and turned to Uncle Fred and the sheriff, whom Uncle Fred had called over.

"We saw some guys in the woods," Pete explained,

"but they weren't spacemen—they just *looked* like spacemen because of what they were wearing."

"And what was that?" the sheriff asked.

"Protective suits," Jill responded. "Like you wear when you're working with dangerous chemicals—"

"And toxic materials," Pete finished for her. By now they had everyone's attention, so they went on to describe all that they had seen. The sheriff listened closely, taking notes and asking several questions.

"Well, well," he said when Jill and Pete had finished, "what do you know? Sounds like there's more to our spacemen stories than we thought."

"Any idea who might be doing the dumping?" Uncle Fred asked. Chris could tell from the controlled tone of his uncle's voice that he was pretty upset. With good reason, too. A lot of the creeks and rivers in the areas were used for irrigation and for watering herds by area farmers and ranchers, like Uncle Fred. If someone was spoiling the water supply, the short-term effects could be disastrous for those who relied on that water for their livelihood. As for the long-term effects on the environment . . . well, Chris didn't even want to think of that!

"No," the sheriff answered, "but I'll sure be checking into it. If I have any more questions for you kids, I'll let you know. Until then, thanks for your help." Jill and Pete nodded, and Uncle Fred ushered everyone back to the pickup.

But as Pete climbed into the truck, he couldn't help wondering if there wasn't something more he could do to

38

help catch the dumpers. In fact, it was constantly on his mind during the busy days that followed.

CHOICE

Turn to page 26.

"There's got to be another answer," Sam said. "We're just not thinking hard enough."

"If I think any harder my brain will explode," Willy said, and the others laughed.

"Well, then you just sit there and let the rest of us do the thinking," Sam retorted. "It's probably safer that way anyway."

"Wait a minute, you guys," Jill said. The others looked at her curiously. She stood and started pacing back and forth. "First," she said in a take-charge voice, "let's consider our options. If Willy can't get out of his commitment, maybe we can get out of ours."

"What do you mean?" Pete asked, starting to feel hopeful. He figured if anyone could find a way around their problem, Jill could. She had a way of thinking things through and coming up with good solutions.

"Chris, did your Uncle Fred say we *had* to come on Friday?"

Chris frowned slightly then shook his head. "No, now that you mention it, he didn't. They don't need to start baling right away. The hay needs to dry for a few days before we could actually bale it. Uncle Fred just thought getting there early would give him some time to show us how to do what needs to be done."

40

"Well, how about if we leave on Saturday morning. That way Willy can still help his mom."

Willy's face brightened. "Hey! That's a great idea. What do you think, guys?"

"Sounds good to me," Pete said. "Since Chris's uncle only lives a few hours away, he could use Saturday afternoon and evening to show us what we need to know."

Chris listened thoughtfully then nodded with a smile. "Sounds like a plan!" he said, slapping Willy on the back with enthusiasm—just as Willy was taking a drink of water. This time Willy saw it coming and took a quick swallow.

"Chris!" everyone exclaimed. Chris looked at Willy sheepishly, then they all broke into laughter.

"Well, now what?" Pete asked when they'd calmed down.

"Now we go find Mr. Whitehead and get things arranged!" Chris said.

CHOICE

Turn to page 18.

"Look, Willy," Chris said. "All you need to do is go ask your mom to let you off this one time. If she says no, then at least you gave it a try."

Willy looked at his friends and nodded then scooted out of the booth. "OK," he said, heading for the door. "I'll see what she says."

All the way home, Willy practiced what he would say to his mom. He even prayed about it, asking God to help him say the right thing. He wanted to sound sincere, but regretful—as though he'd like to stick to his word but it just wasn't going to be possible.

"Yeah, right," he muttered to himself as he pushed open the door and went inside. He walked into the kitchen to get something to drink and stopped cold. His mom was there, seated at the table, looking at a cookbook. He drew a deep breath. Might as well get it over with.

"Uh, Mom . . . ?" he said, and she looked up.

"Oh, Willy, there you are!" she said, a big smile lighting up her face. "Look at this! I found a great bread recipe that we can all make together. We can make small loaves and give them to the nursing home residents. I'm sure they will love them. Everyone enjoys homemade bread. What do you think?"

Willy looked at his mom for a minute, and a question suddenly came into his mind: *Who's going to be more disappointed: you if you can't go to the ranch, or your mom if you don't keep your promise to her?*

No contest, he thought in response. *As much as I want to go to the ranch, Mom would be more disappointed. OK, Lord. You win.*

He went to look over his mom's shoulder at the recipe and picture. He nodded his head.

"Looks great, Mom. And easy. We should be able to get them done in no time." He tried to put some enthusiasm into his voice, but he couldn't. That didn't matter, though. It wasn't going to be fun to keep his word. But it was right. He turned and went to the refrigerator. Maybe a can of soda would make him feel better.

"Willy, what's wrong?"

He looked out from behind the door of the refrigerator. "Wrong? What do you mean?" he asked, trying to sound casual.

His mom smiled a you-can't-fool-me smile. "Honey, I can tell something is on your mind. What's up?"

CHOICE ⇒

If Willy tells his mom what's up, turn to page 135.

If he doesn't tell her, turn to page 122.

It was about nine-fifteen when Pete's phone rang. He chewed double-time on the big chunk of donut he'd just bitten off and grabbed the receiver.

"Hemmo?" he said, trying to talk around the donut.

"Pete? Is that you?" It was Willy. Pete reached for his milk and tried to wash the donut down with a big gulp. He swallowed wrong and coughed and sputtered and gasped for air. On the other end of the phone, it sounded like Pete was under some kind of attack.

"Pete! What's going on? Hello?" Scenes from a television rescue show flashed through Willy's mind. "Pete, raise your hands! Slap yourself on the back! Put your head between your knees! Call 911!"

"How am I supposed to do that with you on the line?" Pete asked, laughing and still coughing slightly. He had finally gotten a breath and had heard Willy's last suggestion.

"Oh," Willy said. Then he grinned. "Yeah, well, I tried to help."

"Thanks a bunch," Pete said. "So what's up? Wait, let me guess. You heard from Chris, right?"

"You got it," Willy said. "Bright and early this morning."

"I thought this was your day to sleep in."

"It was," Willy answered flatly. "So much for that."

"What's this all about, anyway?" Pete asked curiously, and Willy sighed.

"I was hoping you could tell me."

"Nope. No idea. Except that it's 'something great.' I guess we'll just have to go to the Freeze to find out."

"I guess so," Willy said. "See you there."

After they'd hung up, Willy sat down and thought. Knowing Chris, he'd be so excited about his news that he'd forget about their "discussion" this morning. At least, Willy hoped that was the case.

"I guess I'll just have to take my chances," Willy said to himself. "'Cause I'm sure not going to miss out on a Ringers adventure."

CHOICE ⇒

Turn to page 23 to find out what Chris's news is all about.

"**G**ood grief! Look at all these animals!" Tina said, looking around. There were nearly a hundred different animal exhibits to see, with animals of all kinds—horses, dairy cattle, beef cattle, pigs, sheep, goats, chickens, rabbits, and others. The air was filled with noises and smells.

Chris pointed to one of the stalls, where a blue ribbon was proudly displayed on the outside of the stall. "Look, some of the judging has already been done."

Tina looked around. "It looks like a lot of the animals' owners are kids," she said in surprise.

Uncle Fred nodded. "That's true. When you live on a farm or ranch, you start caring for the animals when you're old enough to carry a feed bucket. Lots of kids in the area are members of 4-H clubs or FFA, Future Farmers of America. They raise and show animals as special projects."

"Oh, that would be fun!" Jill said.

"It's a lot of work, too," Aunt Paula added. "I always enjoy seeing how excited the kids at the fair get when their animals win ribbons. They've put a lot of time and effort into them, and it's nice to see them being recognized. There are too many people who have animals and don't care for them."

Chris nodded. "I hate it when people treat animals bad."

"So does God," Uncle Fred said. Chris, Jill, and Tina looked at him curiously.

"Really?" Tina said.

"Of course," Uncle Fred replied. "After all, he told Adam and Eve that they were supposed to take care of the earth and everything in it. That includes the animals. And there are lots of places in the Bible where he told his people to treat animals kindly."

Just then a man called out to Uncle Fred. He turned, saw who it was, and waved. "That's Steve Piter," he said, turning back to Tina and Chris, "a good friend of ours. Aunt Paula and I need to stop over at his dairy cattle exhibit for a minute to see his new friend's calf that's being exhibited. We promised we'd stop by first thing. You can either go along, or we can meet you somewhere. We'll only be there for about fifteen or twenty minutes."

"I'd like to go see the horses," Tina said.

Chris nodded. "Me, too."

"I think I'll go with you," Jill said to Uncle Fred. He glanced at his watch. "OK," he said, "we'll see you near where the horse stalls begin in about twenty minutes." Chris and Tina agreed and took off.

Tina was thrilled at the different kinds of horses on exhibit. There were farm horses like the Morgan horses, and riding horses like the long-legged quarter horses and the smaller, stockier Friesens. There were also some miniature horses there.

"I've seen dogs bigger than these guys," Chris said in amazement, reaching in to pet one of the minis. The miniature horses were only about two and a half feet tall.

"I'd love to take one of these home!" Tina said, scratching one behind the ear.

"So put one in your pocket!" Chris said grinning. They walked around for a few minutes, just looking.

People were standing all around, either looking at the animals or talking. Tina noticed that from time to time people would disappear to an area behind the exhibit stalls. She nudged Chris on the arm.

"What's back there?" she asked. Chris looked up from where he'd been petting a huge pig.

"Did you know pigs have hairs on their snouts?" he asked. "And spots, too! Look at this guy . . . uh, girl," he said when he noticed several little piglets scrambling around.

Tina glanced at the pig then pointed behind the stalls. "What's back there?" she asked again.

Chris shrugged. "I don't know, probably just more animals. Or maybe that's where people keep their stuff." He knelt down to wiggle his fingers at one of the squirming piglets.

Tina wandered toward the back of the exhibits and peeked around the corner. She noticed a horse trailer behind the exhibit stalls. She glanced back at Chris then walked over and looked around.

She noted that the trailer was scratched and dirty, as though it hadn't been taken care of. It smelled bad, too. Tina wrinkled her nose and started to walk away. Suddenly she heard a strange noise. She stopped and frowned.

She cocked her head, listening. Then, she heard it again . . . a whimper! It sounded like an animal . . . in pain.

She walked around the trailer slowly, trying to find the source of the noise. There was nothing there. She listened again then stepped back in surprise. It was coming from inside the trailer.

Tina chewed at her lip, wondering what she should do. She knew she probably shouldn't even be back here let alone trying to get into some smelly old trailer. Maybe she should just go back to the exhibits.

The pitiful whine sounded again, and Tina shook her head. Something was in that trailer, and whatever it was, it was in pain. She couldn't just walk away! Cautiously, she reached out and pulled at the tailgate. It was open. She looked around again then stepped inside.

The filth inside the trailer made the outside look crystal. It was filthy! Tina held her hand over her nose and mouth to avoid breathing in the stench. She peered ahead, trying to see in the dim light that came through the dirty trailer windows. Suddenly she saw something move in the corner of the trailer. She moved closer and felt her stomach lurch. It was a dog—but it was so thin it looked like skin and bones. There was a rope tied around its neck, and the skin under the rope was worn raw.

Tina's stomach turned, and she took another step forward. The dog let out a pitiful sound. It was so weak it could hardly move. It just looked up at Tina and whimpered.

"Oh, you poor thing," she said, her voice choked with tears.

"What are you doing?" a voice asked from behind her.

Startled, Tina whirled around then breathed a sigh of relief. "Man, Chris, you scared me!"

"Serves you right for sneaking around here. Come on, you shouldn't be in here. Besides, this place *stinks!*"

"No, wait," she said. "Come here, Chris. Look at this poor dog!"

Chris came over and Tina heard him draw in his breath. "Oh man! He looks awful!"

"Chris," Tina said, on the verge of tears, "we've got to do something! This poor thing is starving. And look at his neck! We can't just leave him here. Remember what Uncle Fred said? It's our responsibility to take care of the animals."

"Tina, the dog doesn't belong to us. We can't just take it." He looked at the pitiful animal again. "But we can report what we've seen. I bet there are people here who will do something about the dog."

CHOICE ⟹

If Tina and Chris report the abused dog, turn to page 123.

If they take the dog, turn to page 65.

In their panic, they headed straight for the calf, yelling and waving their arms. They spooked the calf all right—straight toward the broken fence! Jill screamed and chased even faster. But the faster they ran, the faster the calf bolted—right toward and finally through the broken fence.

CHOICE

Turn to page 72.

Chris grabbed the fuel can and walked quickly back toward the distiller. He lifted the can, ready to pour the fuel in. Then he stopped. One sentence from Willy's prayer this morning was going through his head. "God, help us to make you proud of us today."

Chris frowned, lowering the can slowly. Sure, he wanted God to be proud of him. But if he did what would make God proud—tell what had happened—would Uncle Fred be disappointed in him? Chris shook his head and lifted the can again, starting to pour. He filled the fuel to the correct level then put the can away. With a last glance at the distiller, he started to walk over toward the others. But as he walked, he felt more and more miserable.

As he came close, he saw Uncle Fred talking to Aunt Paula, a concerned look on his face. "I just don't get it," he was saying, "if I didn't know better, I'd think these critters were drunk! I guess we'd better call the vet."

Chris froze then suddenly made up his mind.

"You won't need the vet, Uncle Fred. At least, I don't think you will,"Chris said. The others all turned to look at him curiously. He felt his face go red. He could still back out. . . . He shook his head and squared his shoulders.

"You were right," he said, looking at Uncle Fred. "The cows *are* drunk. It's my fault. I forgot to check the gas level in the distiller, so when they got their mash this morning, there was more than just mash in it—" He stopped in surprise when Uncle Fred and Aunt Paula both burst into laughter.

"Drunk cattle!" Uncle Fred said. "Now there's one even Sam Babb can't top!"

By now Tina, Willy, and Sam had come over to join the discussion. Their eyes widened when Chris explained what had happened, then they joined in the laughter.

"Maybe you should start your own AA group," Sam said, grinning. "You know, Al-cow-holics Anonymous!"

"Or HH, Hammered Holsteins," Tina added, still laughing. Chris started smiling, too, and soon all of them were laughing so hard there were tears running down their face.

Uncle Fred flashed them a disapproving look, and they said, "Sorry."

Finally Uncle Fred wiped his eyes. "Well, Chris," he said, putting a hand on Chris's shoulder, "thanks for letting me know what was going on. I was getting pretty worried for a minute there. Now, let's see what we can do with these wobbly critters. They still need to be milked, you'll just have to be creative about how you do it."

"And careful, too," Aunt Paula added. "The last thing we want is for one of these tipsy bossies to tip over on one of us as we're milking."

Eventually, it all worked out. They got the cows standing and led them, slowly but surely, into their stalls. There they propped them up carefully and did the milking. There was only one near-incident when a cow that Tina was milking started to sway unsteadily, but Chris and Willy rushed over and stood on opposite sides of the cow, keeping it steady until Tina was done.

"Thanks, guys," Tina said, carrying the bucket over to dump the milk in a large pail.

"No problem!" Willy said with a grin. "We didn't want you getting smashed, too."

Tina and Chris groaned, and Tina grabbed a handful of straw and threw it at Willy. Which triggered a major straw fight that left them all laughing and breathless.

One thing is for sure, Chris thought to himself as he dodged some flying straw, *this trip to the ranch was a **great** idea!*

THE END

Turn to page 14.

Willy went back to sleep and missed the meeting. In fact, he avoided Chris and the others for the next few days. He always managed to be gone when any of them stopped by to see him, and he told his parents he was busy when anyone called. "Just tell them I'll call back," he said. Of course, he didn't. He wanted to make sure that he gave the gang several days to forget whatever Chris had told them about their crazy phone conversation. If there was one thing Willy hated, it was having people make fun of him.

Finally, on the next Saturday morning, Willy went over to the Freeze to see what the gang was going to do over the weekend. But when he got there, no one was around, not even Betty, the owner of the Freeze. Willy figured she must be in the back doing something, so he went to the counter and slid onto a stool. He'd wait for Betty and ask her if she knew where Chris and the others were. The Ringers all considered Betty a good friend, even though she was old enough to be their mom. She always seemed to have time to listen. And she always seemed to have good advice.

Sure enough, a few minutes later Betty came out of the back room. She looked at Willy in surprise.

"Well, what are you doing here? Didn't Chris get in touch with you?" she asked. Willy started to feel uneasy.

"Uh . . . no. Why?" Betty just shook her head, looking at Willy as though she was sorry for him.

"He really has been trying, Willy. I'm sorry. It looks like you've missed the trip." Willy looked at her in confusion.

"Trip? What trip?"

"Chris heard back from his uncle. The work week you all wanted to set up with Chris's uncle on his small ranch came through."

"You're kidding!" Willy said. No wonder Chris had been so excited! But the look on Betty's face crushed any excitement that had started to grow in Willy. She looked so sorry for him that Willy knew something was really wrong. She sighed and shook her head.

"They left earlier this morning, Willy. Mr. Whitehead was driving the whole group up in the church van."

Willy felt as though someone had punched him in the stomach. Hard. The intense disappointment took his breath away. The work week had been *his* idea to begin with! And now he'd missed it. There was no way he could ask Mr. Whitehead to drive back up to the ranch just for him. Especially when it was his own fault that he hadn't found out what was happening.

Betty reached out and patted Willy's hand where it rested on the counter. "I really am sorry, Willy. I know you must be disappointed." Willy nodded. He was too choked up to say anything, though.

"I gotta go," he finally said, and he slid off the stool and headed home. It was too late to do anything about it this time. But Willy knew one thing. He wouldn't ever let this happen again. He'd been wrong to avoid his friends. Even if they *had* made fun of him, it would only have lasted a little while. And being embarrassed for a few minutes sure would have been a lot easier to take than missing what would probably be a week of great adventures.

THE END

Willy's right. He can't go back. But you can! Turn to page 23 to see what would have happened if Willy had gone to the Freeze.

Pete started running. He couldn't take a chance that the truck would be gone. He dodged around people, scanning the colorful carnival booths carefully. Finally, he reached the one he wanted. It was a ring-toss booth, with all kinds of milk bottles set out for people to try throwing rings over.

He took a few minutes to catch his breath, then, as casually as he could he strolled around the booth toward the back. He peeked around just in time to see a man climbing into the truck. He caught a glimpse of the man's face and felt a stab of excitement—it was one of the gun-toting guards from the creek!

The man started up the truck, and Pete scrambled for a better view of the license plate. He felt in all his pockets for a pen and paper but couldn't find any.

"Oh man!" he groaned, "I can't believe this!" Quickly he tried to see the license number but caught only a few of the numbers. Disappointed, he watched the truck pull away and head for the fair exit.

Well, it wasn't what he'd hoped. But at least he could give the sheriff a little more to go on. With a frustrated kick at the ground, he turned and walked back toward the roller coaster to try to find his friends.

58

Turn to page 112.

Willy was startled awake by a terrible noise. He sat bolt upright in bed, clutching his covers and looking around wildly. Chris peered at him sleepily.

"What was that noise?" Willy asked.

"What noise?" Chris said, when it sounded again, right outside their bedroom window.

"*That* noise!" Willy said, jumping up to go look out the window. Chris just laughed and pulled the covers up under his chin.

"That's a ranch alarm," he said. "Better known as a rooster." Right outside their window sat a large, red rooster. As Willy looked on, it took a deep breath, looking a little like a feathered balloon filling up, and let go with another ear-splitting "cock-a-doodle-doo"! Willy shook his head and flopped back onto his bed.

"What time is it?" he asked.

Chris peered at the clock and groaned. "Five-thirty," he said. "In the morning. Welcome to ranch life."

Willy began to wonder if he'd *ever* get to sleep till ten.

Just then there was a tap on the door of their room. "Come on, boys. Time to get up." It was Uncle Fred.

"OK, we're coming," Chris called. Willy threw back the covers and groaned.

"I know he told us last night that we'd be getting up early, but this is insane!"

Chris laughed again. "Actually, he's being pretty nice to us. I'd bet he's been up at least an hour already." Then he sat up and sniffed the air. "Mmmm," he said, mouth starting to water. "And I'd bet Aunt Paula has breakfast all ready!"

Willy sniffed. "Oh boy! Bacon!" he said gleefully, and jumped up to find his clothes.

By the time Chris and Willy staggered into the kitchen, everyone else was there, rubbing their eyes and stuffing eggs, pancakes, biscuits, bacon, preserves, and maple syrup into their mouths. There was fresh orange juice and milk, too. The boys each grabbed a chair and sat down, concentrating on the business at hand: porking out!

"This beats McDonald's hands down!" Pete said, and Aunt Paula laughed.

After breakfast, everyone got ready for church. They all piled into Uncle Fred's extended-cab pickup truck. Jill and Tina opted to sit inside, while most of the guys wanted to sit in the bed of the truck. Since the church was just down the road, Uncle Fred agreed. As they pulled up to the church, Willy and Pete commented on how much it reminded them of their church at home. It was an old, white church with a tall steeple that housed a church bell. There was a boy, who looked to be about the same age as the Ringers, ringing the church bell.

"I wonder who he is," Pete said as he jumped down from the truck bed.

"I don't know," Sam said, looking at Pete sideways, "but his face sure 'rings a bell.'" The others groaned and pushed at Sam, laughing as they approached the church doors.

Inside, the church was beautiful. It had an old-style feel and look to it. "Look at those windows!" Jill said, nudging Willy. He looked up to see beautiful stained glass windows all around the church, each depicting a different scene: the birth of Christ, Jesus being baptized by John the Baptist, Jesus healing someone, Jesus surrounded by children, the Crucifixion, and the Resurrection.

"This place looks like it's been around forever," Sam said quietly.

"Not quite," Uncle Fred commented, "but it has been here for at least 100 years. And there are people here whose great-grandparents built the church and almost everything in it—including those windows."

The Ringers all enjoyed the service. There was a lot of singing, and Uncle Fred and Aunt Paula even sang a duet for special music. Afterward, they all stood outside, talking.

"These must be your new hands," an older man said as he came up to Uncle Fred. He had a big smile and big bushy eyebrows.

"Those look like caterpillars on his forehead!" Sam whispered to Jim, who shushed him quickly.

"Hello, Sam," Uncle Fred said with a smile. "Kids, this is Mr. Babb, one of the elders in the church." Mr. Babb shook everyone's hand as Uncle Fred introduced them.

"Looks like a fine bunch of workers," Mr. Babb said. "I just hope you've told 'em all to keep out of the woods after dark, Fred. I'd hate to have 'em nabbed by the spacemen."

"Now, Sam—" Aunt Paula started to say, but Pete cut her off.

"Spacemen?" he said incredulously. Mr. Babb leaned toward him and waggled his bushy eyebrows.

"All around, boy, in the woods. They've been seen roaming around at night. Heard tell there's even some animals that have turned up missing." The Ringers were all looking from Mr. Babb to Uncle Fred. Was this guy for real?

Uncle Fred just shook his head and laughed. "OK, Sam, you've had your fun. Let's go, kids." They followed him to the truck, but instead of getting in, they surrounded him and bombarded him with questions.

"Was that guy kidding?"

"What did he mean 'spacemen'?"

"Have these 'spacemen' been seen close to your place?"

Finally, Uncle Fred held his hands up in surrender. "Yes, Mr. Babb was kidding," he said. "No, he's not nuts. Several weeks ago some kids came running home at night, scared silly, saying they'd seen some spacemen in the woods. A week or so later, someone called the sheriff to report the same thing: spacemen in the woods. The sheriff checked it out, but of course he didn't find anything in the woods but woods. It's become a joke for some people—they figure they don't need the bogeyman anymore, they've got their very own spacemen. But there are others who are downright upset by the whole thing. They think it makes us look like a bunch of gullible country folk. So it can be a pretty touchy subject.

"Anyway, now that the mystery's been solved, what say we go home for some lunch?"

"All right!" Jim, Willy, and Sam all said, and piled into the back of the truck.

"But the mystery *hasn't* been solved," Pete protested as the truck started up and they headed for the house. "I mean, sure those people didn't see spacemen, but what *did* they see?"

"Who knows?" Chris said. "But it doesn't sound like something we should be digging into. Especially if there are people who don't want to talk about it."

"Yeah," Willy agreed. "Just forget about it, Pete. Besides, we've got more important things to think about. Like how to make room for lunch and more blackberry cobbler!"

Pete settled back, feeling frustrated. *OK, fine,* he thought to himself. *If no one else cares about what's really going on, then neither do I. I'll just stick to mending fences, and the spacemen can take care of themselves.*

The long, relaxed dinner and visits from several neighbors who seemed to be pleased to meet the "kids from town" took up the afternoon. In the evening they returned to church for another service, which included a lot of singing. Then it was back to the ranch for leftovers, stories, and an early lights-out.

Monday morning dawned bright and early. After stoking up on another ranch-style breakfast, the gang gathered in the living room for a group prayer. They stood in a circle and held hands while Willy prayed.

"Lord, please keep us safe today. And help us to do

64

what Uncle Fred and Aunt Paula need us to do to help
them. And God, please help us to make you proud of us
today. Thanks for this chance to be here, God. Amen."

"Amen!" the others echoed and headed for their
assigned projects.

CHOICE ➡

To see how Willy and Sam handle their chores, turn to
page 130.

To find out what Jim, Pete, and Jill do, turn to page 140.

To see how Chris and Tina's chores turn out, turn to
page 99.

Tina stepped forward and knelt down next to the dog.

"What are you doing?" Chris asked.

"I'm not going to leave him here," she said, her voice angry. "We can take him with us to find Uncle Fred." After several hard tugs, she finally had the rope off. She took off her jacket and carefully wrapped it around the dog, then lifted it. It was so thin it hardly weighed anything.

Chris looked to make sure the way was clear. "Let's go," he said, and they stepped out of the trailer. They had only gone a few feet when a man came walking toward them. He was wearing dirty overalls and boots and a dirty baseball hat. Tina shot a frightened look at Chris, who stepped in front of Tina, doing his best to block the man's view of the dog she was carrying. They didn't have to worry, though. The man didn't even glance at them.

As soon as he was past them, they started walking faster.

"Hey!" an angry voice called from behind them. "You kids! You got my dog!"

"Run!" Chris said, grabbing the dog from Tina's arms. They ran out to the exhibit area and looked around frantically. Suddenly Tina shoved Chris toward someone she had picked out in the crowd.

"There's Uncle Fred!" she said. Chris looked behind him just in time to see the dog's owner closing in on them, his face red and angry. Chris ran toward Uncle Fred, Tina close beside him.

Uncle Fred looked up startled when they reached him. "What in the world?"

"It's an abused dog that we found in this guy's trailer—but we couldn't just leave him there so we brought him with us—but the guy came back, and he's after us, and you've just *got* to do something or the dog will die!" Tina said, breathless.

Just then the man rushed up, panting. He made a grab for the dog, but Uncle Fred reached out and caught the man by the wrist. He looked at Uncle Fred angrily.

"That's my dog! Those kids are thieves!" the man said.

"Well, let's just let them tell us what's going on," Uncle Fred said. About that time a man with a judge's badge came walking up.

"What's the trouble, Mr. Chapman?" he asked. Tina was surprised to see the man suddenly look fearful.

"Uh, nothin', Judge. Nothin' at all. Just a misunderstandin'."

"It is *not!*" Tina said, stamping her foot. She was getting even more upset. "That man has almost killed this dog! We found it in his trailer, and *look* at the poor thing!" The judge stepped forward and lifted Tina's jacket, running a hand over the dog. His face was grim when he looked at Mr. Chapman.

"Well, Mr. Chapman?" he said in a cold voice. The man stuttered and stammered, but the judge held up his hand. "Never mind. We'll sort this out back at the official's booth. Right now, I think we need to give this animal some attention." He reached out for the dog, and Chris handed him over. The judge looked at Tina and Chris.

"Thank you for bringing this to our attention. I can assure you that the dog will receive the care he needs. As will Mr. Chapman."

As they watched the judge walk away, followed by a sullen and quiet Mr. Chapman, Tina felt tears running down her checks. Aunt Paula slipped an arm around her shoulders and smiled at her.

"You kids did the right thing," she said. "Come on, let's go enjoy the rest of the fair."

"How can anyone be that mean?" Chris asked.

"It's really not that hard," said Uncle Fred, to the others' surprise. "All you have to do is harden your heart to it."

"Harden your heart?" asked Jill.

"Do it once. Do it twice. Do it a few more times until you don't care anymore. That's how people harden their hearts."

The kids thought about this in silence as they walked through the fairgrounds. They all knew about hardening hearts. Who hasn't hardened his or her heart to something at some time? Suddenly it seemed easier to understand how Mr. Chapman could be cruel to his dog.

"That's why people need Christ, isn't it?" Chris's comment broke the silence and caught everyone's attention. He looked up at Uncle Fred.

Uncle Fred smiled at Chris's insight. "That's exactly right, Chris."

68

Tina watched with mixed emotions as Mr. Chapman disappeared behind another trailer.

THE END

Turn to page 123 for a different twist to this ending.

Turn to page 5 for a different ending to the story.

Or, turn to page 14.

"**L**et's go back to the path," Pete finally said. "We don't really know how much longer these guys are going to be here, and I don't want to take a chance on being here until dark."

"Oh, if only they'd finish—" Jill started to say then broke off at the sound of accelerating engines. She and Pete peeked over the bushes and saw the men retracting the hose. They ducked down again.

"They're finished!" Pete said, excited.

"'Ask and you shall receive,'" Jill quoted again with a grin.

"That's good enough for me," Pete said. "When they leave, all we need to do is follow the tracks their vehicles make. Sooner or later we're bound to come to a road. And then we can find some help."

Within minutes, the men were in the truck and car and moving slowly out of the clearing. Jill and Pete waited a few seconds then quickly followed behind the vehicles.

 **CHOICE**

Turn to page 35.

Jim sat down on the tractor and folded his arms. "OK, have it your way," he said, glancing at the cattle again. "I just think—" and then he stopped. One of the animals was moving—toward the fence.

"Hey," he said, standing up, "I think we've got trouble." Jill and Pete looked where he was pointing.

"Oh, no!" Jill exclaimed. "It's a calf. And it's heading for the broken section of the fence!"

Jim jumped on the tractor and revved it up. Pete and Jill dropped their supplies and started running.

CHOICE ⇒

If the three of them head for the calf, turn to page 50.

If they head for the fence, turn to page 28.

Sam thought for a second then shook his head. "No, thanks, Pastor," he said, smiling at the older man. "I'll be OK." Pastor Whitehead nodded and reached in to pull a suitcase out of the van.

Sam carried his luggage toward the house. He still wasn't real thrilled at the thought of cleaning out the barn. But he'd agreed to come on this trip and help out. He wasn't going to let a little manure stop him from doing what he knew was right. Besides, he'd probably have some really gross stories to tell his sisters when he got home. Stories about being up to his knees in horse crud . . . stories his sisters would hate to listen to!

Hmmm. Maybe this isn't going to be so bad after all, Sam thought. A smile tugged at his lips as he went into the house.

CHOICE

Turn to page 30.

Jim reached the broken fence section first, just in time to watch the calf disappear into the woods on the other side.

"Great!" he muttered. "Just great." Meanwhile Pete and Jill came running up. They had seen the calf bolt through the fence and knew Jim would need help.

"I'm gonna try to catch him!" Pete said, and he ran toward where the calf had entered the woods.

"I'm coming, too," Jill called after him. She turned to Jim quickly. "You wait here, OK? Don't let any other cattle get through. We'll be right back." With that she took off, following Pete.

Jim watched them go, shaking his head. He knew how dense woods could get and how easy it was to get lost. But neither Pete nor Jill had given him a chance to say anything.

"I sure hope they know what they're doing," he said.

More than half an hour later, Jill and Pete still hadn't returned. Jim glanced at his watch and frowned. It was a few minutes to noon, and he knew the others expected them back at the house for lunch. He didn't want to leave. It would be a long walk back for Pete and Jill. Jim was sure they'd be tired after their search in the woods, and they'd be frustrated with him for not waiting. Still . . . what if they were lost?

Maybe the best thing Jim could do was to head back

and let Uncle Fred know what had happened. He would know if they should come back out and look for the lost calf—and the lost Ringers.

If Jim heads for the house, turn to page 129.

If he waits, turn to page 121.

Chris grabbed the fuel can and quickly filled the gas to the proper level. Then he stashed the can and went out to help the others with the cows. After a great deal of struggling, they finally had the cows standing right side up. But Uncle Fred was watching them with a concerned look on his face.

"I think I'll give the vet a call," he said and started for the house. For a minute Chris started to follow him. Then he stopped. He couldn't tell him what he'd done now! It had been bad enough that he'd forgotten about filling the fuel, but covering it only made it worse. Chris turned away angrily, though he wasn't quite sure who he was angry with.

When the vet came to check the cows, Chris made sure he was nowhere around. He kept himself busy doing other chores, such as gathering eggs and feeding horses. He had just finished feeding the last horse when he looked up to see Uncle Fred standing in the doorway of the barn, watching him.

"Uh, hi," Chris said, looking away quickly.

"Hi, there." Uncle Fred's voice was relaxed and friendly.

Maybe he still doesn't know what happened, Chris thought. But his hopes of that went tumbling at Uncle Fred's next words.

"Guess what the doc had to say about the cows?"

Chris swallowed hard then looked up with what he hoped was an innocent look on his face.

"I don't know. What?"

"Are you sure you don't know, Chris?" Chris's eyes fell, and he felt an uncomfortable chill creeping up his neck.

"Well. . . . Yeah. I know. They were drunk, right?"

"Right you are," was Uncle Fred's only reply. Chris looked up at him.

"I'm sorry, Uncle Fred. I should have told you what happened. But I felt bad about forgetting the fuel in the distiller. Then when I tried to cover up what I'd done . . . well . . . things just kind of got away from me."

Uncle Fred nodded understandingly. "I know, Chris. Things have a way of doing that. But I do wish you would have told us. It costs us a good bit of money to have the vet come out here. If we'd known what had happened, we could have avoided that expense."

Chris looked at his uncle. "I'll pay you back," he said, his voice shaking a little. Chris had no idea how much a vet visit cost, but he figured it couldn't be *that* much.

Uncle Fred smiled at him and shook his head. "That's not necessary, Chris," he said, then he grinned. "Besides, I'd hate to be responsible for you being without an allowance for the next six months."

"Six months!" Chris gasped. Then he squared his shoulders. "Well, if that's what it takes, then that's what it takes. I should pay for the vet since it was my fault he had to come."

76

Chris looked his uncle square in the eye and thought he saw him holding back a smile. Uncle Fred nodded, then put his hand out, and they shook on it. "OK, Chris," Uncle Fred said, "if that's how you want it. We'll talk with your folks and work out the details. And thanks. Every little bit helps when you're trying to get by on a ranch."

"You're welcome," Chris said, feeling warm inside. "I'll just finish up these chores and come in the house in a minute."

After Uncle Fred left, Chris sighed. *Six months of allowance! Ouch!* Then he smiled and shook his head. Regardless of how hard it would be, the sacrifice was worth it to regain his uncle's—and his own—respect.

THE END
Turn to page 14.

Chris took the note from his uncle, folded it up, and slipped it into his pocket. "I guess if you can't go, you can't go," he said, his voice heavy with disappointment. "But it sure won't be the same without you."

Pete nodded. "I agree with Chris. Maybe we should think this whole thing over some more."

"Maybe we can contact Uncle Fred and see about going a different week," Jill suggested. Chris looked at her, then nodded slowly.

"I can do that—"

"Gee, you guys," Willy said. "I don't want you to cancel the trip. I mean, the group has done other things before without *everyone* going. You know I'd like to go, but this time I can't."

"I think we've all figured that out by now, Willy," Chris snapped. Willy looked at Chris, surprised and hurt by his response. Chris looked down, feeling ashamed but frustrated. Why did Willy have to mess everything up? "Look," Chris said gruffly, "I'll talk to you guys later." With that he turned and hurried out of the Freeze.

The rest of the gang sat in startled silence, watching him go. Finally, Jill reached over to pat Willy on the arm.

"Don't worry about it, Willy," she said. "Chris will come back. And we'll work it out."

"Yeah," Pete agreed. "You did what you had to do. You couldn't just back out on your mom."

Willy nodded. He knew he'd done the right thing, he just wished it felt better. "Sometimes," he muttered, "doing the right thing really stinks."

"That's just because there are so many of us who'd rather do what *we* want than what God wants," Betty said quietly. The group looked at her, surprised. They hadn't realized she was listening.

"I saw the way Chris left and figured something was wrong," she said with a wry smile. Willy nodded sadly.

"I figured he'd understand," Willy said, feeling a little angry himself.

"Well, we all get upset about things at times," Betty said. "Even when it doesn't make a whole lot of sense. I'm sure Chris will realize you did what was right, and he'll be back."

"Yeah, Willy," Pete said, "it's really no big deal. Chris just acted dumb because he was disappointed. When he comes back we can just tell him we forgive him for being such a dope."

"Right," Sam agreed. "And then we can figure out when we *all* can go on this work week. It can't be that hard to come up with a week we can all go."

Willy sighed, then he nodded. "OK," he said, then he smiled. "In the meantime, I think I need a milkshake."

"Now *there's* a good idea," Pete said, reaching for the menu.

As the gang placed their orders for their second round of ice cream creations, Willy settled back in his seat. He was sorry Chris had gotten so upset—but he was glad Betty and the others had been there to keep him from getting mad back.

At least now, he thought to himself, his mouth beginning to water as Betty set his double-chocolate milkshake in front of him, *if and when Chris does come back, I won't be mad at him. And maybe we'll be able to work out the trip after all.* With that encouraging thought, he took a big sip of his shake.

THE END
But it doesn't have to be the end for you! Turn to page 39 to continue the homestead adventure!

Or, turn to page 14.

"**O**K, OK," Chris said, setting down the paper he'd been waving. "You win. Give me the dumb washcloth."

Betty smiled at him tolerantly. Pete reached out and took the paper Chris had set down, glancing at it curiously. It was a letter.

"You missed a spot," Jill said sweetly, pointing to a blob of chocolate sauce. She was enjoying watching one of the guys do the cleaning up for a change. As one of the two girl members of the Ringers, she'd gotten cleaning duty more often than she liked.

"Hey," Pete said suddenly, "this is a letter from your uncle!"

"Oh, yeah!" Chris said, dropping the washcloth and snatching the letter from Pete. "He sent me an answer to our letter about the work week!"

"All right!" the others chorused. Several weeks back, the gang had talked with Mr. Whitehead about putting together a work project where they could help someone out for a week during their summer break. Chris had suggested contacting his uncle, who lived on a small ranch. He explained that it was time for his uncle to harvest his small crop of hay. He'd already cut the hay, but he'd told Chris he would be glad to have help baling it—in addition to a long list of other projects that needed to be done: fixing fences, helping gather the strays from his herd of cattle, painting some of the buildings, and other chores. Since Chris's uncle and aunt had no children, they usually did the work on the ranch themselves. They almost always could use extra help. The group had agreed to offer their services for a week.

"So what's the news?" Willy asked, now as excited as Chris.

"Uncle Fred wants us to come!" Chris exclaimed. "He says he's got plenty of things for us to do and that we could be a big help to him and Aunt Paula."

"That's great," Jill said. "When do we leave?"

"Next Friday!" Chris answered with a grin. "Is that soon enough for you?"

"All right!" everyone exclaimed in excitement.

Everyone, that is, except Willy. He just looked down at the table, disappointment written across his face.

Chris frowned. "What's up, Willy?"

Willy sighed as the others looked at him curiously. "I can't go on Friday. I promised my mom I'd go with her to visit a nursing home on Friday."

"Can't you get out of it?" Pete asked. "How important can visiting a nursing home be?"

"For my mom, *real* important," Willy said. "It's something she's done ever since my grandfather had to be in a nursing home. It really bothered her how few people came to visit the other residents there. So ever since then, she visits one of the nursing homes in our area once a week. She takes cookies and books and stuff and spends time talking with as many people as she can—even the ones who don't seem to know she's there."

82

"That's nice," Jill said. But Chris just frowned again.

"So can't you go with your mom some other week?" he asked. "I mean, well, you really wanted to go to the ranch, and it *was* kind of your idea to begin with, and . . . well, it just wouldn't be the same without you," he finished, starting to feel miserable himself.

Willy looked at Chris doubtfully. "I don't know, Chris. My mom depends on my sisters and me to go with her. She says we can visit more people that way and that the people at the homes really like talking to us—you know, to young people. And both of my sisters are going to be gone next week. So if I don't go, my mom goes by herself. Besides, I promised."

CHOICE ➡

If Willy sticks to his promise, turn to page 97.

If he tries to go on the trip, turn to page 41.

Pete and Jill looked around, slightly confused. Jill knew they'd been to this part of the woods before, but she couldn't quite place it. They had lost the calf long ago. Now they were just trying to find their way back to Jim and the fence. Unfortunately, neither Jill nor Pete had paid attention to where they were running when they were chasing the calf. When they'd started back, they never found the fence.

Jill glanced at her watch. They'd been wandering around for more than an hour! "Pete," she said, looking around and sounding worried, "are you sure we aren't just walking in circles? Everything looks the same after a while."

Pete glanced at Jill, then looked around him again. "No . . . ," he said slowly, "I'm not sure. But I don't think so. Let's just keep following the path. If we don't come out someplace in another half hour or so, then we'll have to try to figure something else out."

Jill nodded and fell into step beside him. They had only walked a little further when Pete suddenly stopped. Jill looked at him in surprise.

"What—?" she started to ask, but he held up his hand for her to be quiet. He stood for a moment, listening.

"Listen," he finally said, "do you hear something strange?"

Jill strained to listen carefully. She *did* hear

something. At first she thought it was just water running, like a rushing creek or a small river. Then she detected something else . . . something mechanical, like a motor running.

"Yes," she said, feeling excited. "It sounds like some kind of machine running. I think it's coming from over there," and she pointed through the trees beside them. Pete followed her pointing finger, considering the downward slope of the ground, the denseness of the trees, and the thick undergrowth. They could get through, but it wouldn't be easy.

He sighed in frustration. They could stay on the path they'd found, but he was almost sure they were going the wrong direction. They could try to find whatever was making the noise, but there was no guarantee that anyone would be there to help them. And they'd just be deeper in the woods.

If they stay on the path, turn to page 6.

If they follow the sound, turn to page 92.

"**C**ome on, Pete," Willy said coaxingly. "It's not that bad. It'll be a good experience."

"I'll get sick," Pete said flatly.

"No way!" Willy said, and Pete had to admit he sounded convincing. "Besides, just think how good it will feel to be able to say you really did it, you rode the Demon!"

Finally, Pete gave in. "OK, I'll go," he said, sounding like someone who'd just agreed to step in front of a firing squad. Willy, Jim, and Sam talked and laughed the whole time they were in line. Pete just got quieter and quieter. When they finally climbed into a car and pulled the safety bar back, Pete felt beads of sweat on his forehead.

"You're gonna love this!" Willy said gleefully, clamping a hand down on Pete's shoulder and startling him. If he hadn't been strapped in, he would have jumped ten feet in the air.

The climb to the top of the first downhill ramp seemed to take forever. At least, that's how long Pete hoped it would take. He scrunched down in his seat, praying he would survive with dignity. Then the cars crested the top of the metal hill. Pete peeked through his fingers, which were clamped firmly and protectively over his eyes, and saw that there was no bottom. He opened his mouth to protest . . . to ask politely if he could get off now

. . . to tell Jim and Willy that he was going to make them suffer for putting him through this. . . .

But just then they started their first plunge, and all that came out of Pete's terror-frozen lips was a very sincere, *"Aaaauggggh!"*

Forget dignity! He just wanted to get out of this with his life!

It was only a few minutes later that the cars came to a stop and the ride was over. Willy, Sam, and Jim jumped out of the car, laughing and slapping each other on the back. They had walked several feet before they realized that Pete wasn't with them. They look back and saw him bent over next to a nearby bush.

"Uh oh," Jim said, sympathy struggling with laughter. "Looks like our buddy really shouldn't have gone on the ride." They waited quietly for Pete, who eventually joined them, his face a peculiar shade of green.

Wisely, Jim, Sam, and Willy kept silent.

"I went on your *stupid* roller coaster," Pete finally said in a low voice. Jim and Willy nodded. "Don't ever ask me to do that again."

More nods and a muttered, "OK."

Willy slipped a cautious arm around his friend's shoulders. "But, you know, now that you've really gone on one," he said, trying to sound encouraging, "it wouldn't be so bad to go again, would it?" Pete's glare cut through him. Willy removed his arm.

"Uh, yeah, right . . . never again. Got it," Willy mumbled. *Sheesh!* Some people just didn't appreciate the ways friends could broaden their horizons.

THE END

Turn to page 14.

Sam looked at Mr. Whitehead and nodded. The older man smiled at him then called to the others that they would be back in a few minutes.

"Let's go over here," he said, and they started out. With a glance at the others, Sam fell into step beside the man. He shoved his hands into his pockets and kicked at a rock angrily. Mr. Whitehead didn't say anything. He just waited until Sam was ready to talk.

"I'm not sure I want to stay here," Sam finally said.

"Oh? Why is that?"

"Well . . . " Sam hesitated, then rushed on. "Nobody said anything about shoveling out any barns! I don't want to be walking and working in that stuff. I mean, it's OK for the others, they don't seem to care one way or the other. But why should I have to do something like that? It's—it's gross!"

Mr. Whitehead stopped walking and looked at Sam. "Sam, I know being on a ranch is different for you. You're right, the others have been in places like this before, but it's new to you. If there are some things you don't want to do while you're here, I'm sure you could just say so. It sounds as though there is plenty of work to do. Then again, you might want to give yourself a chance to try some new things. You might even find out that they're not as bad as you think."

Sam thought for a minute. Maybe Mr. Whitehead was right. Maybe things wouldn't be all that bad. . . . But what if they were? What if he got stuck doing the really crummy jobs and hated every minute of it?

Sam shook his head. "I just don't want to stay," he said stubbornly.

Mr. Whitehead nodded. "OK, Sam. It's your choice. You can go back home with me. When we get back to the van, you'll need to go to the house and call your parents to let them know you're coming."

They turned to head back to the van. When they got there they saw that the luggage was all unloaded and sitting on the ground. The other Ringers were hauling it into the ranch house. Sam reached out and stopped Pete just as he picked up one of Sam's bags.

"It's OK, Sam, I've got it," Pete said.

But Sam shook his head. "It doesn't go in the house," he told Pete. "It goes back in the van."

Pete looked at him in surprise.

"Back in the van?" Willy asked, coming up beside them. "Why?" Sam wished he could just leave without telling anyone, but the whole group was gathering. He shoved his hands into his pockets.

"I'm not gonna stay," Sam said, somewhat defiantly. The others looked at him, shocked. Sam held up his hand as they started to protest. "Look," he said, "I'm not gonna argue with you guys. I don't want to stay. You guys said this was all volunteer work, right? Well, I've just changed my mind. I don't want to volunteer, OK? So I'm going back home. End of story. That's it."

"Now wait a minute . . . ," Chris started to say, anger building inside him. But a voice from behind him stopped him.

"Hang on, Chris." It was Uncle Fred. "Your friend is right. This is a volunteer work week. And if Sam has decided he doesn't want to stay, that's his choice."

"Yeah, but—" Chris started to protest, but his uncle just smiled at him.

"Chris, ranch life isn't for everyone. You may enjoy being here, but not everyone does. And that's OK. Sam isn't hurting our feelings. We trust God to help you and your friends to make the right decisions for yourselves."

Jill nodded. "That's true, Chris. It's up to each of us to stay. We can't make Sam stay if he doesn't want to." She turned to Sam with a smile of understanding. "Sam, I really wish you would stay. But if you don't want to, then that's OK with me. It's up to you." The others murmured their agreement, and Sam looked down at the ground.

"I don't know what to do," he finally said, feeling miserable.

"I'll tell you what, Sam," Uncle Fred said after a minute. "How about we make a deal?"

Sam looked up at him curiously. "A deal?" he asked.

Uncle Fred nodded. "How about you agree to stay for a day or so. If you decide after that time that you still don't want to be here, you can call your parents and have them pick you up."

"That's a good idea," Willy said.

"Come on, Sam," Tina said hopefully. "Just give it a try." Sam looked at his friends, then at Mr. Whitehead.

"It's up to you, Sam," he said. "But I'll guarantee you—you may work hard, but you will *not* get bored."

"That's right," said Chris.

"Especially with us around," added Willy.

CHOICE ⇒

If Sam goes back home, turn to page 127.

If he accepts Uncle Fred's offer, turn to page 9.

"I think you're right," Pete said. "Let's go check it out. Maybe there will be someone there who can show us how to get back to the road."

They made their way through the trees, pushing the thick bushes aside and stepping carefully. Finally, they came to the edge of the woods. Pete paused and Jill glanced around him at the clearing. She saw a small meadow. The creek she had heard ran alongside the far end of the meadow. And there, next to the creek, she saw something surprising.

"A dairy truck?" she said, looking at Pete curiously. "What's a dairy truck doing out here in the middle of nowhere?"

"Yeah, well, what I want to know," Pete said in a hushed voice, "is what those refugees from a spaceship are doing out here!"

Jill looked again and saw that Pete was right! There, next to the truck, were several men in what appeared to be some kind of hooded outfits that completely covered them from head to foot. They had strange-looking contraptions on their faces, too. Like some kind of gas mask with two small canisters coming out at angles in the front. They looked like big white beetles.

"Looks like we've found the mysterious 'spacemen,'" Jill said. "But they're not from Mars. They're from . . . " She squinted her eyes to read the name on the side of the dairy truck. "Shelman's Dairy Farm." She looked at Pete and noticed he was frowning.

"I think I've seen suits like those someplace," Pete muttered. Jill shook her head. She'd never seen anything like them before. Besides, she didn't feel like standing in the woods and playing guessing games. There was only one way to find out what was going on. She started to push the bushes aside and walk out, but she was suddenly jerked backward. Pete grabbed her arm and pulled her down.

She looked at him in surprise. "What are you doing?" she asked angrily.

"Where are you *going?*" he demanded.

Jill shook her arm free. "Where else? To ask those guys where we are and how to get back to the road!"

Pete frowned at her. "I don't think that's such a good idea, Jill," he said. "Have you noticed what those guys are carrying? She looked in the direction of his nod and saw something she hadn't noticed before. There were several other men leaning against a nearby car. They weren't in the strange suits. They were wearing business suits—and holding shotguns.

"What's going on here?" Jill asked, her voice a little shaky.

"I don't know," Pete answered. "But those guys with the guns sure aren't hunters. They look more like lookouts or guards of some sort." He glanced back at the truck. "What could that truck be doing way out here that would require guards with guns? I'm gonna see if I can get closer."

Jill hesitated. It would be pretty hard to move around without making noise because of all the brush around them. What if they were spotted? The last thing she wanted was to be shot at! She realized the sound of the creek and the truck had so far kept them from being discovered.

CHOICE

If Jill stays where she is, turn to page 111.

If she follows Pete, turn to page 15.

"I have an idea," Pete said after a few moments. Jill looked at him expectantly. "I don't know if you're going to like it. . . ."

"Are you going to say we should walk up to these armed space weirdos and ask them for help?" she asked.

"No way!" he answered.

"Do you think we should just sit here all night until someone comes to find us, provided that we don't die of exposure or get eaten by wolves or some other hungry wild animal?"

Pete felt a smile tugging at his mouth. "No."

"Do you think we should wait for the bozos with the guns to leave, then go taste the water just to see if the stuff they're dumping is really toxic?"

"Definitely not."

"OK, then, I'll like your idea," Jill said with a nod.

Pete grinned at her. He had to admit it, if he had to be stuck in a fix like this with a girl, he was glad it was Jill. "OK, here's the plan. We wait until these guys are done with whatever they're doing, then we follow them out of the woods."

Jill frowned. "How will we keep up with them? That truck and car can go a lot faster than we can."

"That doesn't matter, not in these dense woods. All we have to do is follow the tracks they make. Sooner or later, we'll find a road. And once we do that, we should be able to see where we are. Even if nothing looks familiar, I'll bet we can find a house or a phone."

Jill nodded. "OK. Sounds good. I just hope we don't have to wait too long for these guys to finish—" She cut off at the sound of an engine accelerating. She and Pete looked at the truck and saw that the men were retracting the hose. They were done!

"'Ask and you shall receive,'" Pete quoted with a grin. Within minutes, the men were in the truck and car and moving slowly out of the clearing. Jill and Pete waited a few seconds, then quietly followed the vehicles. They made sure they stayed out of the drivers' line of sight, going parallel to the vehicles' tracks rather than directly behind them. That made the going a little more difficult, but they managed.

Turn to page 35.

Willy thought about the problem for a few moments, then shook his head decisively.

"It's not going to work," he said with a sigh. "I can't really ask my mom to change her plans; it would be too hard. And I can't ask her to go without me; that wouldn't be fair. So I guess you'll just have to go on the work week without me." He gave the others a slightly crooked, sad smile.

"I don't know, Willy," Chris said, disappointed. "This whole thing was kind of your idea to start with. I'd hate to see you not go."

Willy nodded. He wasn't real thrilled with the idea of being home while everyone else was gone, either. He looked around the table at his friends and shrugged his shoulders.

"I don't know what else to do," he said.

CHOICE ➤

If the gang gets frustrated with the situation, turn to page 77.

If they try to think of a solution, turn to page 39.

98

Jim looked at Pete. "I know it would be a long walk for you guys," he said softly. "But Uncle Fred asked us to make sure we didn't let any of the cattle get through the fence if we could stop them. I just don't want to take a chance. If I can block the hole in the fence, I'll come back for you."

Jill stood up, wiping sweat from her forehead. "Pete, I think Jim's right."

"OK, OK," he said. "Go ahead, Jim. We'll catch up to you when we're done."

Jim jumped onto the tractor and revved it up. As he started toward the broken section of fence, he kept glancing at the cattle nervously. Unfortunately, the sound of the tractor startled them, and a couple of the younger calves bolted, heading for the fence.

"Oh no!" Jim yelled. He put in the throttle to make the tractor go as fast as it could. The trailer bounced along behind him, tossing the supplies all around. But Jim didn't even notice. All he saw was one of the calves making a beeline toward the broken fence.

Make that *through* the broken fence.

CHOICE

Turn to page 72.

Chris, Tina, and Aunt Paula walked to the milking barn. They had already fed the cattle before breakfast, using the mash from the fuel distiller. Chris was humming to himself, looking forward to milking the cows. He remembered how much fun that had been when he'd visited before. Suddenly, Aunt Paula stopped in her tracks.

"Oh my goodness!" she said. Chris and Tina followed the direction of her stare, and their eyes widened in disbelief. There in the field was a cow lying down. The mere fact that it was lying down wasn't all that strange—cows often sleep lying down. But cows hardly ever lie on their backs . . . with all four feet up in the air! That's exactly what this cow was doing. Aunt Paula hurried forward with Chris and Tina close behind. As they reached the cow, they realized that there, among the bales of hay that were set out for the cattle to munch on, were several other cattle in the same upended position.

"What in the world . . . ?" Aunt Paula said, then she turned and hurried back to the house to get Uncle Fred. Tina and Chris just stood there, not sure if they should laugh or be upset. Actually, it was a pretty hilarious sight! The two Ringers found themselves struggling to control their laughter.

"Upside-down cows!" Tina said, stifling a giggle. "Now I've seen everything!"

"I sure hope they're not sick," Chris said, looking around. Just then he noticed another cow walking toward them . . . or, rather, trying to walk toward them. With each step it became apparent that the animal's legs were too wobbly for it to go in a straight line!

"That goofy thing walks like it's drunk!" Tina said. Chris started to laugh—then he froze. *Like it was drunk*. . . .

"Ohmigosh!" he said. He glanced at Tina. She was busy trying to get one of the upside-down cows turned right-side-up. He looked all around to be sure no one was watching, then sprinted for the distiller.

He skidded to a halt, then dropped down to check the gas level on the distiller. It was empty. Chris shook his head in dismay. He'd forgotten to keep the gas filled! Without fuel, the alcohol hadn't been burned off or distilled into the fuel. Instead, some of it had gotten into the corn mash, which they'd fed to the cattle, which were now drunk.

Chris looked around quickly. By now, Uncle Fred, Aunt Paula, Tina, Sam, and Willy were all out trying to get the plastered Holsteins back on their feet. They weren't having much luck. They'd get one up, but when they left it to head over to another cow, the standing bovine would slither back down to the ground. Uncle Fred had pulled some of the hay bales over, using them to prop up the wobbly cows. But as Chris watched, one of the other cattle, which apparently was either recovered or hadn't eaten enough of the mash to be affected, came over and started pulling at the hay for some breakfast. Sure enough, when the sober cow tugged at the hay, the bale moved, and the propped-up cow slid back to the ground with a pitiful moo.

Chris swallowed hard. He glanced at the others again, just to be sure no one noticed where he was. Then he started toward the gas. If he could fill the distiller now, nobody would have to know what had happened.

CHOICE ⟹

If Chris decides to fill the fuel and not tell his aunt and uncle what happened, turn to page 74.

If he decides to tell them what happened, turn to page 51.

The next several days of baling went quickly. In fact, they finished baling the hay a day sooner than Uncle Fred had expected. So he decided to get a head start on spreading manure on the now-harvested field.

"Spreading manure?" Sam said in a feeble voice.

"Sure," Uncle Fred told him as he hooked the manure spreader up to the tractor. The spreader looked like a long, two-wheeled cart with a conveyor belt that went down the middle of the bed. A metal bar with "fingers" stretched across the back end of the spreader.

"How does this thing work?" Willy asked, looking at it curiously.

"Actually, it's very simple," Uncle Fred said after he'd pulled the spreader up next to a pile of manure. "First, we load it." And with that he handed Willy and Sam shovels.

"Ugh!" Sam said, looking at the pile and wrinkling his nose. But Willy didn't even hesitate. He went over and started shoveling. Sam held back for a minute then went to help. He shoveled carefully, making sure not to spill anything and trying to breathe through his mouth.

"I'll say one thing for you, Sam," Uncle Fred said with a grin. "You're the neatest shoveler I've ever seen!"

Once the spreader was loaded, Uncle Fred drove it to the field.

"Who wants to drive?" he asked, and Sam stepped

forward quickly. He figured the safest place to be was in the driver's seat! Uncle Fred showed both Sam and Willy how to start the conveyor belt.

"See?" he said. "The belt moves the manure toward the metal fingers, and they flip it out of the cart onto the field."

"No problem," Sam said. "It works like a salt spreader, and I've worked with those before." He was starting to feel better about the whole thing. The stuff still smelled rotten—but at least he wasn't going to have to touch it!

Uncle Fred just smiled, and he and Willy stepped back as Sam started out.

"Uh, Uncle Fred?" Willy said, standing with his arms crossed and watching Sam as he bumped along on the tractor.

"Hmmm?"

"What Sam said about this thing working like a salt spreader. Is he right?"

Uncle Fred's grin grew wider, and he glanced at Willy, his eyes twinkling. "Well . . . all except for one little detail," he said.

"What detail?"

"Salt spreaders shoot the salt out nice and neat. Manure spreaders, on the other hand, toss manure wherever and whenever they can."

Willy's eyes grew big, and he quickly looked at Sam. "So sitting on the tractor doesn't mean you won't—"

"Get a little on you? Nope, it doesn't mean that at all. But you know the old saying, don't you?"

Willy frowned. "What saying?"

"You're not really a rancher until you've tiptoed through the cow patties. I figured we owed Sam that enriching experience . . . "

Just then, Sam glanced over at Willy and Uncle Fred. He had a big grin on his face. Yes, sir! He was getting to like this ranching stuff. In fact, it was even fun . . .

Plop!

Something had hit his shoulder. Sam looked down, startled. "What . . . ?" His eyes widened in stunned disbelief as he stared at the big chunk of cow dung that had just done a perfect one-point landing on his shoulder.

"Auuughh!" he yelled, trying to brush it off, which got it all over his hands and his arm—and a little in his hair. He jumped off the tractor frantically (which, fortunately for him, shut off automatically when the driver got down) and hopped around, brushing at himself, shaking his hands, and yelling.

That was when he heard it. Hoots of laughter. He looked up to see both Willy and Uncle Fred laughing so hard they had to hold on to each other to keep from falling over.

"Hey, Sam," Willy called gleefully, "how's it feel to be a *real* rancher?" Sam's eyes narrowed dangerously. He looked at the spreader, then back at the two who were still bent over in laughter.

Setting his jaw, he did the only honorable thing he could do. He hopped over to the spreader, took two handfuls of manure, and headed for his two "friends." Before they realized what was happening, they found themselves under attack. Sam gave a victory yelp when one handful hit square on the side of Willy's head.

With a wicked grin, he ran back toward the spreader for more ammo, Willy and Uncle Fred hot on his heels.

Later, after they'd finally gotten cleaned up—outside with the hose—they had a great time telling anyone and everyone about what had happened. Veterans of a manure fight love to tell their stories. And everyone else loves to hear them.

Except for Sam's sisters.

So Sam pleaded with his friends. *"Please,* you guys, let *me* tell them what happened." They finally agreed.

And any last bit of horror Sam felt from his experience was forgotten in his delight when his sisters ran from the room, holding their hands over their mouths, calling him "the grossest brother in human history!"

Now *that* was worth suffering for.

THE END

Don't want the adventure to be over? Go back to page 59 and make different choices along the way.

Or, turn to page 14.

Tension hung thick in the air. The only sound in the Freeze at that moment was the drip of the spilled milkshake still answering gravity's call from the table to the floor.

"Considering that you're the one who *caused* the mess to begin with," Jill said, "you just seemed the likeliest candidate to clean it up."

"*I* caused it?" Chris said. "No way! I'm not the one who turned into Mt. Vesuvius and spouted chocolate all over everywhere. And Jill and Pete knocked their own stuff over—I didn't even touch the table!"

Willy glared at him. "Yeah, right, Chris!" he said, anger tinging his words. "Like you had nothing to do with it!"

"Whoa, now, hold everything you guys," Betty said, setting the bowl of water and the washcloth on a nearby table. "Before you get all upset over this, what say we decide this the democratic way?"

The friends all looked at her curiously. "The democratic way, eh?" Pete said thoughtfully. "What do you mean?"

"Simple," Betty said with a smile. "We were all here, and we all saw what happened, right?"

"Right," everyone chorused.

"So, we simply decide by a show of hands who we think should clean the table up. Majority rules."

"Wait a minute," Chris protested. "That's not fair!"

Betty looked at him thoughtfully. "Why not, Chris?"

"Yeah, why not?" Willy demanded. Chris felt himself turning red again.

"Well, because they'll all say it was my fault, and all I did was hit Willy on the back. I couldn't help it that he was taking a bite when I did it."

"But it was your slap on the back that caused the problem?" Betty asked, still looking thoughtful.

"Well . . . yeah, but. . . ." Chris paused, trying to think of something to say. But Betty was right. It *was* his slap that made Willy choke. And if he hadn't choked, the others wouldn't have ducked, so the milkshake and soda wouldn't have gotten knocked over. . . .

Chris sighed. He hated it when other people were right. Especially when that meant *he* was wrong.

CHOICE

Turn to page 80.

Several hours later, Sam walked into the room where Willy was resting. Willy's attack had been severe, probably the worst he'd ever had. The doctor had been pretty concerned when he arrived. He finally gave Willy some kind of cortisone pill, telling Uncle Fred that if Willy didn't respond soon to the medication, they'd have to take him to the hospital. Fortunately, the pill had worked. Now Willy was lying down, letting his system recover from the assault of the asthma and the medication.

Sam pulled up a chair and sat next to the bed. Willy smiled at him weakly.

"Hey there," he said, his voice still pretty weak and breathless. His hands shook as he reached up to adjust his pillow. He grimaced. "I feel like I've had about twenty cans of super-caffeine cola," he said.

"The doctor said the medication he gave you would probably make you a little hyper and shaky for a while," Sam said. They sat for a moment in silence. "I hear your mom is coming to pick you up," Sam finally said. Willy nodded. Then they both started to talk at the same time. "Sam, I'm sorry, I should have told Uncle Fred. . . ." "Willy, I'm sorry. I should have done something sooner. . . ."

They both broke off then laughed. Sam shook his head.

"I'm real sorry you have to go home, Willy," he said.

"Me, too," Willy answered. "But the doctor said it will probably be a few days before I'm back to normal anyway—not that I was ever normal to begin with," he finished in a rush to beat Sam, who had opened his mouth to say the same thing. Sam grinned then looked down at the floor.

"You know, Willy, I didn't think you were gonna make it," he said quietly.

"Me, either," Willy said.

"I mean, you weren't breathing, man. Sheesh, you scared the corpuscles out of me." Sam shook his head, upset with himself. "I should have told Uncle Fred, no matter *what* you said."

"But Sam, it was my fault, not yours. I knew better—but I just didn't want to miss out on anything," he shook his head. "I never thought it would hit me *that* bad. But as soon as Uncle Fred said there would be a lot of dust, I should have said something. I was lucky I got off as easy as I did—"

"Luck had nothing to do with it," a voice broke in from the doorway. Sam and Willy looked up to see the other Ringers standing there. "As I was saying," Chris continued as they came into the room, "luck didn't take care of you."

"I know," Willy said. "God did."

"See?" Chris said looking around at the others, with satisfaction. "I told you he was smarter than he looked."

"Thanks, Chris," Willy said wryly. "I think."

As the Ringers laughed, Willy looked at them and smiled. He would miss not being on the ranch for the rest of the week . . . and he hated to miss out on the adventures he knew his friends were bound to have.

Maybe next time.

THE END

What if Willy and Sam had done things differently? Turn back to page 130 to see what else could have happened.

Or, turn to page 14.

In frustration Jill sat down.

Crack! She jumped. She had sat back on a brittle branch! Frantically she looked toward the guards. They were looking around, suddenly suspicious. One man signaled for the others to look around, and they began to walk right toward where Jill was hiding.

She crouched low to the ground and carefully backed her way deeper into the woods, praying that the men couldn't hear her over the sound of the truck's pump. She went what she thought was a safe distance, and hid behind a large bush. She listened for footsteps coming toward her and sighed in relief when she didn't hear anything.

After a few minutes, she headed in the direction Pete had gone. No way she was going to stay by herself now!

CHOICE

Turn to page 15.

Several weeks later, as the Ringers were gathered around a picnic table for a lunch break outside the Freeze, Uncle Fred and Aunt Paula surprised them by driving up in their pickup.

The gang greeted them as they got out.

"We were in town to visit Chris's mom, and we heard you were here," said Uncle Fred. "We wanted to let you young detectives know that your tip about the milk truck paid off."

"No kidding?" Pete said. "What happened?"

"Well, they traced the name you saw on the dairy truck. Seems it belonged to a dairy that went out of business a year ago or so. They located the owners and investigated the different people who purchased their trucks. And they hit the jackpot—found that a local chemical company had bought several of the trucks. They contacted the EPA at that point and let them take the investigation from there. They tested the water from that creek, and it contained waste materials that matched those coming from the chemical plant. There's a full-fledged investigation underway now, and it looks as though the plant is in for some hefty fines, and it may even be closed down."

The Ringers all listened wide-eyed. "Wow," Sam said with a low whistle. "That's great!"

"Well, it's a start, anyway," said Uncle Fred. "But the hardest part is still coming."

"Why's that?" Tina asked.

"Because the EPA and the investigators have to determine how long the dumping has been taking place, and what kind of damage the area has suffered, and all that sort of thing."

"You mean the water and the soil?" Pete asked.

"Even more than that. There may have been some damage to people as well. In addition to being in the water and soil, the toxins are also carried in the air. Which means people probably have been breathing in stuff that could have done some pretty serious damage. There's no telling right now how far-reaching the effects of the dumped chemicals are. We'll have to wait and see."

Uncle Fred smiled at the suddenly somber group in front of him. "Hey, I didn't mean to spoil your lunch! I just wanted to tell you kids thanks for your help and congratulations on catching some criminals! Oh, and I wanted to drop these off." He passed out some booklets he'd been holding. "They're from the EPA. They figured you kids might enjoy them."

"Thanks, Uncle Fred," said Willy.

"Why do people do things like that, Uncle Fred?" Chris asked.

"There are lots of reasons, Chris," answered Aunt Paula. "Proper disposal of toxic wastes can get pretty expensive, especially for older companies that don't have the right equipment or facilities. Some companies decide to dump waste illegally rather than spend the money to have it taken care of correctly. Some companies are concerned about inspections and being fined."

"Well, I think those companies ought to be shut down!" Tina declared.

"I think something needs to be done about the people, not the companies," Jim said, almost to himself. The others looked at him curiously.

"What do you mean?" Jill asked.

"I just figure that companies are run by people—you know, the managers and owners and stuff. And they're supported by people, too—by people like us who buy their stuff. So if anything is really going to change, I just think it has to start with people changing. Like us."

"Yeah, but we don't dump toxic wastes!" Sam protested.

"That's true, Sam," Aunt Paula said, "but we can do something about the people who do. I think Jim has the right idea. By telling Sheriff Wilson what they saw, Jill and Pete helped to stop the illegal dumping. But we can do even more than that. We can make sure *we* don't contribute to the waste problems, too."

"Hey, I know what you're talking about," Chris jumped in. "You're talking about recycling and that kind of stuff!"

Aunt Paula smiled. "That's exactly what I'm talking about."

"We recycle," Tina said. "We save soda cans and bottles and paper and aluminum foil—"

"And a partridge in a pear tree!" Willy finished with a chuckle.

Tina stuck her tongue out at him. "Very funny! But I'll bet I know something you don't," she said, holding one of the booklets Uncle Fred had passed around.

"You're on!" Willy said. "Let's hear it."

"How much energy do you waste when you throw away two aluminum cans?"

"Two cans, huh? Let's see, multiply the cans by kilowatts, then divide by nanoparsecs to the second power. . . ."

Tina punched his arm. "Just admit you don't know."

Willy shrugged. "OK. I don't know. Illumine me, O wise can woman."

"When you throw away two aluminum cans, you waste more energy than one *billion* of the world's poorest people use in a day," Tina said.

"Two cans?" Jim said. "Come on, Tina. That can't be right!"

"Well, that's what it says here!"

Uncle Fred smiled at Jim's astonishment. "When you get down to it," he said, "it's pretty mind boggling how much we affect the world. We're only one species on the planet, but we do seem to have a well-developed ability to destroy."

"Whoa!" Jim exclaimed, "listen to this. Did you know that fifty acres of rain forest are destroyed every minute, that one-tenth of the oil that's produced in the world will end up in the ocean, that if you lined up all the styrofoam cups made in just one day they would circle the planet, that—"

"Enough already!" Willy said, grabbing the booklet.

Sam put his elbows on the table and leaned his chin on his hands. "So how do we stop affecting the world?" he asked.

Uncle Fred smiled. "Well, you don't. You learn how to affect it in better ways."

"Maybe that could be the Ringers next project," Aunt Paula said as she started to clear the table. Tina, Sam, and Jill jumped up to help her.

"Hmmm," Willy said thoughtfully, reaching for a booklet. "Maybe we *could* do something."

"Yeah?" Pete said as he and Chris looked over Willy's shoulder. "Like what?"

"Like turning off lights when we leave a room," Willy said, reading as he paged through, "or not using styrofoam cups, or supporting a local zoo, or cutting apart six-pack holders, or—"

"OK, OK," Pete said, holding his hands up in surrender. "So our next assignment will be to save the earth."

"At least to save our part of it," Willy said, grinning. "I mean, hey, that's a start, isn't it?"

"Sounds like a plan to me!" Chris said, "but I think *I* should be the brains of the operation." And with that he grabbed the booklet from Willy and took off running, with Willy and Pete hot on his heels.

THE END
Turn to page 143.

"**U**ncle Fred," Sam finally said, "Willy's got something he wants to tell you." Willy looked at Sam, startled, then felt his face turning red as Uncle Fred looked at him inquiringly.

"Yes, Willy?" he said. Willy cleared his throat and kicked at the ground.

"I, well, that is . . . oh, crud. I've got asthma." Uncle Fred looked at Willy, surprise on his face.

"Asthma? Well now, that could be a problem, son. Do you have a very bad case of it?"

Willy looked at him, feeling miserable. "I guess so, I mean, well, yes. But I carry my inhaler with me, and it doesn't usually cause me too much trouble as long as I'm not in a lot of dust and stuff. . . . " Willy's voice trailed off. Uncle Fred looked at him for a minute then made a decision.

"Tell you what, Willy," he said. "I've got some paint/dust masks in the barn. If you think you want to give this a try, you can wear one of the masks and see how it goes. We'll take a couple along so you can switch them when one gets too dirty. But the minute you feel any reaction—and I mean the minute you feel it—you boys let me know. I don't want you getting into trouble with your breathing. OK?"

Willy nodded, relieved. "OK," he said. Uncle Fred

headed for the barn, and Willy turned to Sam, who was looking half guilty, half defiant.

"I'm sorry, Willy," he said quickly. "I just didn't want to take any chances—"

Willy shook his head. "It's OK, Sam," he said. "I understand. Besides, you're right. It's better to be honest about what's going on . . . and the last thing I need is to get an attack out in the middle of a hayfield."

Uncle Fred came back and showed Willy how to put the mask over the lower part of his face, and they left for the field. Soon everything was set, and the boys were busy hauling and stacking the bales of hay.

When they started out, the dust wasn't too bad. But it wasn't too long until even Sam had to pull out his neckerchief and put it over his nose and mouth. He watched Willy closely and was relieved to see that he seemed to be handling the dust well—thanks to the mask.

The machines made a lot of noise, though, so they had to yell to hear each other over the machines. They started out taking turns grabbing the bales as they fell into the wagon and hauling them to the far end. Then they tried using a kind of relay system. Willy would grab a bale when it was dropped into the wagon, lift it, and toss it as best he could toward Sam. Sam would then lift it and stack it. They worked this way for the rest of the afternoon, switching places from time to time.

When the wagon was full, they unhooked it from the baler and hooked it up to another tractor. Willy drove the tractor up to the barn, where he, Uncle Fred, and Sam unloaded the bales and stacked them. Then they went back to the field and went to it again.

The boys were grateful when lunchtime came, and they were ready to kiss the ground when the work day was finally over. Uncle Fred had apparently neglected to mention a few of the finer points of baling hay—like the fact that their arms would feel like they weighed about two tons at the end of the day, or that they would be covered with dust and chaff before the day was over, or that they'd feel like someone had doused them in itching powder!

Willy dragged himself to his room, wondering if he could stay awake long enough to eat dinner. He had just managed to take off his shirt—quite a feat since he couldn't lift his arms any higher than his shoulders—when Chris came bursting into the room.

"Boy, what a day this has been!" Chris said with enthusiasm. "We had a blast!" Chris slapped Willy on the back. "Too bad we've only got three more work days left, huh, Willy?"

Willy, who had sprawled in agony—facedown—on his bed when Chris slapped his back, lifted his head just enough to glare murderously at his friend.

Chris glanced at him. "Hey, Willy, I don't think there's time for a nap before dinner," he said, grabbing a towel. "But if you're going to lie down, you won't mind if I jump in the shower first. Thanks, pal!" And with that he was gone.

With a muffled groan, Willy dropped his head back down on the bed, wondering if he would suffocate before

120

he managed to move—and trying to decide which he'd rather do.

"Oh boy, only free more dayff . . . ," he muttered into the bed. "If I could liff my armf, I'd drown you, Chrif."

Turn to page 102.

"I'd better just wait," Jim said to himself, then settled back on the seat of the tractor. But it wasn't long until the midday sun made him feel as though he was going to melt. He wiped his forehead and reached for the lemonade. Rats! The jug was empty. He rummaged around in the trailer, looking for something else to drink. But there was nothing.

He glanced around. There were no shade trees, except for the woods. And he had to stay out here to keep any other cattle from getting through. Well, one thing was certain. He couldn't stay here for very long. He'd turn into a crispy critter in no time!

CHOICE

Turn to page 129.

Willy looked at his mom, then just smiled. "It's nothing, Mom. Really."

His mom looked at him curiously then reached over to pat him on the shoulder. "Well, if you say so, Willy. I trust you. Now, when shall we get started with making the bread?"

A little later, Willy sat in his room, thinking. He had called Chris and told him he wouldn't be going on the trip. Through Chris had been disappointed, Willy knew he understood. The others would understand, too.

And though Willy would miss out on this adventure, he knew there would be plenty of other opportunities in the future. *After all,* Willy thought with a grin, *adventure seems to follow us Ringers everywhere we go!*

THE END

Willy may have to wait for the next Ringer's escapade, but you don't! Turn to page 135 to continue the adventure.

Or, turn to page 14.

Chris reached out to take Tina's arm. "Come on," he said softly. "Let's go find Uncle Fred. He'll know what to do."

Reluctantly, Tina followed Chris out of the trailer. They stopped long enough to copy the license number, then ran back to the horse exhibits. It wasn't long before they spotted Uncle Fred, Aunt Paula, and Jill at one of the stalls, talking with an owner. They ran up to them.

"Uncle Fred," Tina said urgently, "can we talk to you?"

"Sure, Tina," he said. He followed them a little distance away, and they described what they had found. Uncle Fred frowned then walked back over to his friend. After a few minutes of talking, Uncle Fred, Aunt Paula, and Jill came back.

"Come on, kids. Mr. Piter, our friend over there, told us who we should report this to."

"But what if someone comes while we're gone and moves the trailer?" Tina protested. Uncle Fred paused for a minute, then Aunt Paula touched his arm.

"Chris, Jill, and I can go to the official's booth. Why don't you and Tina go back to the trailer and wait for us. We'll come as quickly as we can."

Chris, Jill, and Aunt Paula hurried away, and Tina and Uncle Fred went back to the trailer. They stepped inside and went over to the dog, who quivered violently as they approached.

"Tina," Uncle Fred said, "you'd better just hang back. The dog may be weak, but that's no guarantee that it won't bite." Cautiously, he stepped toward the dog. It lifted it's head for a second, then dropped it back in the filthy straw. Uncle Fred knelt beside the dog and reached out to pet it gently, speaking softly.

Suddenly an angry voice came from behind them. "What's goin' on here! What do you think yer doin'?" They looked up to see a man standing there, his hands on his hips.

"Are you the owner of this dog?" Uncle Fred asked. Tina was surprised to hear anger in Uncle Fred's voice, too.

"What if I am?" the man spat out.

"Then you've got some things to answer for," Uncle Fred, replied. "This animal has been starved and beaten."

"It's my dog, I'll do with it what I want!" the man said, then started to come forward. But he stopped when Uncle Fred stood. Tina smiled. Apparently the man hadn't realized how big Uncle Fred was.

Just then Tina heard Chris's voice. "It's over here, Mr. Clark." Within seconds, Chris and a tall gentleman with a judge's badge were looking into the trailer. The owner of the trailer looked at them startled and tried to close the door.

"There's nothin' in there to interest you," he said gruffly.

The judge reached out to stop him. "I'll decide that, Mr. Chapman. Please step aside." The man stepped back sullenly, and the judge came to kneel beside the dog, running his hand over the animal's side and haunches. With a grim expression, the judge untied the rope from around the dog's neck. Chris stepped forward, holding out a small blanket that he'd found. The judge wrapped the blanket around the dog and lifted it carefully. When they stepped out of the trailer, he fixed the man with an angry stare.

"Mr. Chapman, this dog is being confiscated. You will please accompany me back to the official's booth where we can discuss the animal's care and fate. I can assure you that your chances of getting him back are slim—as are your chances of being allowed to show any other animals in this competition. The sheriff will also want to inspect your other livestock. Apparently you have forgotten how to care for your animals properly. We will do all we can to remind you."

As Chris and Tina watched them walk away, Tina felt tears running down her checks. Aunt Paula slipped an arm around her shoulders and smiled at her.

"You kids did the right thing," she said. "I'm sure the dog will be all right once given the proper care."

"How can anyone be that mean?" Jill asked.

Uncle Fred put a hand on her shoulder. "It's kind of like we discussed earlier. It's our responsibility to take care of the earth and the animals on it. Some people just don't believe that. They don't want to put out the energy or money."

"They should take all of his animals away!" Tina said.

"They'll take away any that aren't being cared for

properly," Aunt Paula told her. "And they'll be watching him from now on to be sure he doesn't make the same mistakes."

"Thanks to Tina and Chris," Uncle Fred said. "Too many people would have just decided it wasn't their business and left the dog to its fate. But you two cared enough to do something. Come on," Uncle Fred said. "I think it's time to get you animal champions some ice cream."

THE END

Turn to page 143.

Sam thought for a minute then shook his head. "I appreciate your offer, Mr. Martin," he said to Uncle Fred. "But I really just want to go home."

Uncle Fred nodded understandingly. "I'm sure you know what's best for yourself," he said. "Maybe the group will decide to come again, and you can come then. You're always welcome."

Though the others were disappointed, they tried to be supportive of Sam and his decision. They knew it hadn't been easy for him. They just wished he'd decided to stay.

As the van pulled away from the ranch, Sam sat in the passenger's seat, staring out the window. He didn't say much on the trip home. He just sat, feeling miserable. He'd thought that once he was on his way home, he'd feel better. But he didn't. If anything, he felt worse.

"I really let everyone down," he said, breaking the silence.

"You did what you felt you needed to do, Sam," Mr. Whitehead responded.

"Yeah, but they were counting on me to help out."

"Yes, they were," Mr. Whitehead agreed. "But they'll make out all right." Sam just turned his head toward the side window, fighting the tears that stung at his eyes.

"Sam," Mr. Whitehead's voice was kind, "we all make decisions we regret. It's a part of being human. We don't

128

always know what's right or wrong. Sometimes we just have to choose and then learn from what happens—and pray that God will teach us. The important thing isn't whether you made a mistake, but admitting you blew it and learning what you can from it. And making it right if you need to."

Sam looked at him. "How can I make this right again? I can't go back to the ranch—we're almost home. So what can I do?"

"That's a question you'll have to answer for yourself," Mr. Whitehead said. "But a good place to start may be to apologize to those you disappointed. You can tell the others what you've realized when they get home. And you can talk to God about it whenever you're ready."

Sam nodded. That was true. And there was something else he could do, too. He could pray that God would let his friends have a great time on the ranch, that he would keep them safe, and that they would get all the work done. Maybe he would even write them a letter while they were at the ranch to tell them he was sorry.

It wouldn't change what he had done. But it would be the right thing to do.

THE END

If you want to see what would have happened if Sam decided to stay, turn to page 9.

Or, turn to page 14.

Finally, Jim reached a decision. He pulled a couple of boards out of the trailer and quickly nailed them over the broken section of fence.

"That should keep any other cattle from getting through," he said when he'd finished. Then he got on the tractor and started it up. With a last glance at the woods, he turned the tractor toward the house.

"I'll go nice and slow," he said to himself. "That way, they can catch up with me if they come back soon."

But they didn't come back, and before long Jim pulled the tractor up next to the barn.

"Hey! Where have you been?" It was Chris. He was sitting in a chair on the porch. "We've been waiting for you guys. Lunch is ready, and . . . Hey, where are Pete and Jill?"

"I don't know . . . well, not for sure, anyway. They took off into the woods. I think they may be lost."

Surprise and then concern showed on Chris's face. The woods could be dangerous.

"Come on," he said, opening the door for Jim. "We'd better go tell Uncle Fred."

Turn to page 83.

Sam and Willy watched and listened with interest as Uncle Fred hooked the baler to the tractor and then the hay wagon to the back of the baler. He explained that when the tractor started moving, it would set the baler in motion, scooping up the cut hay, which was lying in rows. Once inside the baler, the hay was dumped into a sort of funnel where it was compressed into rectangle-shaped bales. When a bale reached the right size, the baler would tie it with twine, then push it out of the baler through a chute and into the hay wagon. There, Willy and Sam would be waiting to stack the bales, each of which would weigh from sixty-five to ninety pounds, toward the back of the wagon. Once the hay wagon was full, they would hook it onto another tractor and head for the hay barn to stack the bales there.

"So all we have to do is stack the bales? Hey, no problem!" Willy said with confidence.

"Yeah, that sounds real easy," Sam agreed.

Uncle Fred looked at them and smiled. "I'm glad you boys feel that way," he said as he headed for the tractor. He came back a few seconds later with two neckerchiefs. He handed them to the boys.

"What are these for?" Willy asked curiously.

"To put over your mouths and noses when the dust gets too bad," Uncle Fred said.

Sam looked at Willy in alarm. "The dust?" he asked.

Uncle Fred nodded. "Sometimes it can get pretty thick back there. It's not dangerous, but it can make breathing difficult. Well, you boys just relax for a few minutes, OK? I'm going to go get a thermos of lemonade from Paula, and we'll be on our way."

Sam started to say something, but Willy stopped him. As soon as Uncle Fred was out of earshot, Sam spoke up. "You can't do this, Willy!" he said in concern. "What about your asthma?"

Willy frowned. "Don't worry about it," he said. "I've got my inhaler with me. I'll be fine."

"I don't know—" Sam started to protest.

Willy shushed him. "Uncle Fred's coming back. Trust me, Sam. I know what I'm doing."

Sam looked at his friend, feeling worried and frustrated. He knew Willy hated being limited by his asthma. He could understand that—he wouldn't like to have to limit the things he did, either. But he remembered being with Willy once when he'd had an attack, and it had been pretty scary.

"OK, boys," Uncle Fred said, reaching into the hay wagon and setting the thermos in a corner. "We're off! Any questions before we go?"

Sam looked at Willy, then at Uncle Fred.

132

CHOICE ➡

If Sam doesn't say anything about Willy's asthma, turn to page 137.

If he decides to tell Uncle Fred, turn to page 117.

"**L**ook, guys, I don't want to go on that. Why don't you just go ahead, and I'll wait."

Willy reached out and grabbed Jim and Sam by their sleeves. "Come on," he said, pulling them toward the line. "You and I can die by ourselves! Pete will have a front-row seat. Right, Pete?"

Pete looked at Willy gratefully and nodded. Then he looked around and spotted the ride he'd been looking for. "Hey, you guys," he yelled. "I'm going on the Ferris wheel. I'll meet you back here."

"You got it, dude," Willy called back.

Pete stood in line then finally climbed into one of the gently swinging seats. As the wheel began to turn, he craned his neck to see all that he could. It was on about the third time around that he glanced toward the carnival booths and noticed . . . a dairy truck! A truck just like the one they'd seen in the woods was parked behind one of the booths! He waited for the next revolution of the wheel to make sure. Yep, it was the same kind of truck!

He made a mental note of the booth the truck was behind. As soon as the wheel came to a stop, he jumped out of the seat and took off. He'd only gone a few steps when he remembered that he was supposed to be meeting the others. But what if someone moved the truck while he was waiting?

134

CHOICE ⟸

If Pete waits for his friends, turn to page 10.

If he goes on without his friends, turn to page 57.

Willy closed the refrigerator and went to sit by his mom. He filled her in on what was happening, explaining his struggle in making the right decision.

"I really don't want to let you down, Mom," he said softly. "But I don't want to miss the trip, either." His mother watched him, a thoughtful look on her face. After a minute or so, she got up.

"Willy," she said, "you wait right here." And with that she left the room. It wasn't more than ten minutes before she returned.

"Son, I have some good news and some bad news," she said teasingly.

Willy looked up at her, a smile tugging at his mouth. "What's the bad news?" he asked.

"You will have to stay here and help me out on Friday," she answered. His smile faded with his hope as she dropped into the chair beside him and put her arm around his shoulders. "Don't you want to hear the good news?" she asked, that teasing note still in her voice.

Willy looked at her curiously. "Sure, Mom. What's the good news?" he said obligingly.

"The good news is that the group won't be leaving for the ranch until Saturday morning. So you can go with them." Willy blinked in surprise, looked at his mom in

136

stunned silence for a minute, then whooped in excitement
and threw his arms around her for a bear hug.

She laughed and hugged him back. She explained
that she had called Mr. Whitehead to ask his advice, and he
had told her that Jim and Tina couldn't go until Saturday,
either. So they'd called Chris's uncle, and he'd said that was
fine. Everyone could just come on Saturday.

Willy's mom leaned over and gave him a quick kiss.
He was in such a good mood, he didn't even complain.

"I'm proud of you, Son," his mom said. "You made
the right choice by sticking by your promise to me. I'm just
glad that it worked out so you could go."

Willy smiled. "Me too, Mom."

CHOICE

Turn to page 18.

Sam started to open his mouth, then clamped it shut. If Willy wasn't going to say anything, he wouldn't either. He didn't want to get Willy mad at him. Besides, Willy was old enough to take care of himself.

When they started out, the dust wasn't too bad. There was a lot of noise, so they had to yell to hear each other over the machines. Then when the bales started coming, they got too busy to talk much. They started out taking turns grabbing the bales as they fell into the wagon and hauling them to the far end. Then they tried using a kind of relay system. Willy would grab a bale when it was dropped into the wagon, lift it and toss it as best he could toward Sam. He would then lift it and stack it.

They had been working this way for almost an hour when Sam noticed that Willy was slowing down. He looked at his friend in concern.

"Are you OK?" he yelled over the roar of the baler. Willy looked at him and nodded, but Sam noticed that his friend was breathing a lot harder than he was. He reached into his pocket and drew out the neckerchief Uncle Fred had given him.

"I think we'd better put these on," he yelled, holding it up. Willy nodded, and they each tied one around their face so that it protected their nose and mouth. Thankfully, that seemed to help. At least, Sam thought it did. But it wasn't much longer before he noticed that Willy was leaning over, resting his hands on his knees, a pained look on his face.

"Willy!" Sam said in alarm and rushed over to his friend. When he reached him he could hear how ragged Willy's breathing was.

"Oh man! Where's your inhaler?" Sam asked urgently, and Willy reached into his back pocket and pulled it out. Just then another bale shot into the hay wagon, knocking into Willy and sending his inhaler flying.

"Oh no!" he cried breathlessly, and Sam saw panic on his friend's face. He dove to where he thought the inhaler had landed and began searching frantically among the hay and dust. Willy slumped against the side of the wagon, then slid to his knees, trying to breathe.

Just when he'd almost given up, Sam saw the inhaler and grabbed at it. He thrust it into Willy's hand, then catapulted himself over the side of the hay wagon and sprinted toward the tractor, yelling to Uncle Fred to stop. Uncle Fred looked around in alarm, stopped the tractor, then came running. By the time he and Sam reached the wagon, Willy was sitting, leaning back with his eyes closed, drawing in ragged breaths. Sam was shocked to see that Willy's lips were slightly blue.

"He's got asthma," Sam said, his voice shaking.

"Asthma!" Uncle Fred said, looking from one boy to the other. "Boys, why didn't you tell me?" He jumped into the wagon and loosened Willy's shirt collar. He noticed the inhaler in Willy's hand.

"Did you use this?" he asked Willy urgently. Willy nodded weakly. "How many times?" Uncle Fred asked.

"Twice," Willy managed to say in a whisper.

"That's all you can use this for now," Uncle Fred said, his voice grave. "Sam, we'd better get him back to the house." Sam could only nod miserably as Uncle Fred lifted Willy and climbed out of the wagon carefully. "Sam, run ahead and have Paula call the doctor, *fast!* I'll unhook the tractor, and we'll be right there."

Sam took off toward the house, running as fast as he could and praying all the way that Willy would be all right.

CHOICE

Turn to page 108.

Pete, Jim, and Jill headed for the barn. They loaded their tools and supplies into the trailer, just as Uncle Fred had shown them.

"It's a good thing we're finally starting to work," Jim said, patting his stomach. "After the meals we've been having, I think I've gained ten pounds already!"

"Speaking of meals," Jill commented as she set cans of paint in the trailer, "Aunt Paula said we should plan on coming back for lunch around noon."

"OK," Pete replied.

"She also gave us some lemonade and iced tea to take along," Jill continued. "She seemed pretty sure we'd want it before too long."

Jim looked at the sky and pushed back his straw hat. It was a hat he'd brought with him from Brazil the last time he was there. "She's probably right," he said. "It's pretty warm already. I'll bet it's going to be royally hot today." He looked at Pete as he came walking up, his copy of the map in hand.

"I don't suppose you happen to know where there's shade?" Jim asked him.

Pete grinned and shook his head. "Nope, but if we get too warm, I figure we can send you out as a scout. You grew up where it was hot and muggy, so you should be used to it. Besides, you're dressed for the part," he said, flicking a finger at Jim's hat. "All you need is a feather to stick in the band!"

"Hey, great idea," Jill said, laughing. She ran over to the chicken coop and came back with several colorful feathers in her hand. Jim grinned at her good-naturedly, held out his hand for a feather, and stuck it in his hatband.

A few minutes later they were on their way, Jim driving the tractor and Jill and Pete riding in the trailer with the tools and supplies. They followed the fence, watching carefully. They found several damaged sections of fence, and they went to work.

Pete had been a little worried that the day would drag, but when he looked at his watch after what had seemed a short time, he was surprised to discover that it was already after eleven o'clock. Sweat was dripping from his forehead and stinging his eyes.

"Whew!" he said, reaching for the jug of lemonade in the trailer. "This is hard work."

"I'll say," Jim agreed, flopping down on the ground. "This could take forever to get all of this fence done!"

"Hey, we've gotten a lot done so far," Jill said, looking up from where she was painting a replacement board. "I think we can make it to the end of this section before lunch." Pete and Jim looked at her, then at the fence.

"Maybe," Jim said, not sounding too convinced. "Hey," he continued, pointing, "there's some of Uncle Fred's cattle." The others looked up. Sure enough, about a quarter mile away there was a small group of cattle. As they watched the animals, Jim looked along the fence.

Suddenly he noticed a section of the fence that was completely broken apart.

"There a real bad section up there," he said, pointing at it. "Maybe I should go on ahead and start repairing it while you guys finish here."

"Nah," Pete told him. "I don't want to walk all the way over there to catch up with you. Just hold on, and we'll be done here soon."

"I don't know, Pete," Jim said doubtfully. "That fence is completely broken apart. There's nothing to stop one of those cows or calves from going through and heading into the woods."

Pete looked up at his friend, impatience showing on his face. "Come on, Jim. We're not going to take that long. Just wait for us."

CHOICE ⇒

If Jim goes ahead to fix the fence, turn to page 98.

If he waits for the others, turn to page 70.

The Ringers' trip to the ranch held some surprises for them, didn't it? If you haven't followed all the different choices they *could* have made, turn back to the beginning and see what else could have happened!

Make sure you don't miss their other adventures, either. Willy, Sam, Jill, Pete, Chris, and Tina have many other exploits in the *Choice Adventures* series!

For more information on saving the earth, your local library is an excellent source. Just ask the reference librarian for information on the environment or pollution, and he or she will know what's most up to date. You can also check a bookstore.

Karen Ball is associate editor and line manager for children's, youth, and fiction books at Tyndale House Publishers. She has also served as a youth sponsor at her church. Karen lives with her husband, Don, in Aurora, Illinois.